A Candlelight Ecstasy Romance®

"ARE YOU MERELY AN IMPUDENT CHILD— OR A WOMAN I SHOULD BE WARY OF, PIPPA?"

There was a quality to his voice that made a shiver run up her spine. Pippa forced herself to appear unruffled. "How could I pose any threat to you?"

"Very easily." Something flared very briefly in his eyes, then was gone, as though a curtain dropped. "I came here on business, not pleasure. Don't tell me you're like all the others, fascinated by what I have for breakfast?"

"No, and I'm not going to hide under your bed either."

Jeremy's voice deepened to a husky pitch. "That's good. I'm finding, much to my surprise, that I'd rather have you in it."

The glow in his eyes lit an answering warmth in the pit of her stomach. Pippa caught her breath. "I think I'd better be leaving."

"You're probably right," he answered absently, his eyes on her full mouth.

Pippa was powerless to move. Every instinct told her to head for the door, but she was caught in the web of his magnetism, drawn toward Jeremy Hawke by a force as old as nature itself. . . .

D1281733

A CANDLELIGHT ECSTASY ROMANCE®

A RISK
WORTH TAKING

Jan Stuart

Published by
Dell Publishing Co., Inc.
1 Dag Hammarskjold Plaza
New York, New York 10017

Dell ® TM 681510, Dell Publishing Co., Inc.

Candlelight Ecstasy Romance®, 1,203,540, is a registered
trademark of Dell Publishing Co., Inc., New York, New York.

ISBN: 0-440-17449-X

Printed in the United States of America
First printing—July 1984

To Our Readers:

We have been delighted with your enthusiastic response to Candlelight Ecstasy Romances®, and we thank you for the interest you have shown in this exciting series.

In the upcoming months we will continue to present the distinctive sensuous love stories you have come to expect only from Ecstasy. We look forward to bringing you many more books from your favorite authors and also the very finest work from new authors of contemporary romantic fiction.

As always, we are striving to present the unique, absorbing love stories that you enjoy most—books that are more than ordinary romance.

Your suggestions and comments are always welcome. Please write to us at the address below.

Sincerely,

The Editors
Candlelight Romances
1 Dag Hammarskjold Plaza
New York, New York 10017

CHAPTER ONE

The newsroom was quiet after the frantic rush that always preceded air time. Tonight had been especially hectic since one writer was on vacation and another had called in sick.

Pippa Alcott was taking a well-earned breather, her long, slim legs propped up on a chair. The respite lasted only until the UPI broadcast wire in the corner sounded a clarion call.

Pippa's blue eyes narrowed in concentration as she counted. Four bells—that meant urgent. Hurrying to the chattering machine, she read the bulletin swiftly before ripping off the copy. Her typewriter made the staccato sound of a machine gun for a few moments. Each line of large-size type meant one second of air time, so Pippa condensed it as much as possible. This was a late-breaking bulletin, not a regular news story.

She crossed the courtyard at a trot, heading for the control room—which was referred to simply as "the booth" by everyone who worked there.

Without glancing at the multiple television screens that filled one complete wall, she went to a counter stretching almost the length of the room. As she rapidly ripped the colored sheets apart, a man slouched in one of the chairs behind the counter eyed her mockingly. He was handsome in a rather dissipated way, but there was a discontented droop to his mouth, and his pouched eyes were hard.

"Well, well, if it isn't our little star reporter, here with another hot flash," he drawled.

"It's dirty work, but somebody has to do it," she mocked back at him, her hands deftly separating the multiple sheets.

Before Pippa was hired six months ago, Woody Phelan was considered the top news writer at KCTV for the Los Angeles station's award-winning six o'clock news show. He still held that opinion; however, it was no longer shared by everyone. Pippa was now the rising star.

In a short space of time she was rapidly making a name for herself in broadcasting circles. She had a solid background in investigative reporting, and had paid her dues by working her way up in newspapers and magazines.

She had been forced to fight for everything she got, partly because of her appearance. It was Pippa's cross to bear that she looked years younger than her actual twenty-five, especially when she was dressed casually.

It might have helped if she had cut the long, sun-streaked mane of light brown hair that rippled around her slim shoulders, but she stubbornly resisted. What was the use? There would always be some male editors who never looked beyond her slender, curved body and flawless features. When they discovered the keen mind behind those limpid blue eyes, it invariably came as a shock. Pippa had become adept at fending off passes and patronage alike. She had taken it all in stride, letting her work speak for itself until gradually the disparagement turned to respect.

Woody's attitude was one she had encountered many times, so she didn't let it bother her. In addition to being a male chauvinist, he was lazy and not overly scrupulous. It was Pippa's opinion that he had taken credit for many another reporter's legwork, but she was more than a match for him.

Picking up the sheets of paper, she distributed one each

to the producer and the director, two of the four men who sat in front of a bewildering array of electronic equipment facing the wall of television screens. Another copy would go into the TelePrompTer, and the remaining one to the anchorman in the studio around the corner.

The producer, Ray Martindale, was on the wall phone that connected with the studio. He held out his hand. "Something hot, Pippa?"

"Freight train derailed outside of Pittsburgh, suspected sabotage," she said tersely.

"Cue the live remote," the director ordered. "Camera two, zoom in for tight shot of Hawke coming out of the plane."

Pippa glanced up at the bank of TV screens, seeing different shots of Jeremy Hawke descending the steps of a 747. "He looks more like a movie star than a government investigator," she murmured.

"Don't sell him short," Ray answered. "I hear he has one of the shrewdest minds around. He's one of those electronics wizards, the hotshot geniuses who become millionaires before they are thirty,"

"He can't be too bright to go work for the government as an unpaid consultant." Woody's disparaging voice came from the background.

By common accord, Pippa and the producer ignored Woody, watching the tall, lean man stride onto the tarmac. A crowd of reporters and cameramen surrounded him, running to keep up with his fast pace.

A microphone was thrust in his face as someone shouted, "Does the government suspect there were kickbacks involved in awarding the contract for Evergreen Elementary?"

The wide, generous mouth formed a thin line in Jeremy Hawke's strong face. "That's your supposition, not mine."

"Well, then, do you think the contractor used inferior material?" another voice called.

"I have no evidence to that effect." Hawke's light eyes were expressionless, his deep voice carefully guarded.

"If you were sent out from Washington to investigate, you must have *some* suspicion of wrongdoing," a reporter commented.

They had reached the terminal. Jeremy Hawke turned, his broad shoulders towering over the group crowding around him. Impatiently brushing away a lock of dark hair he said, "Evergreen Elementary School was partially funded by the government. That's why I'm here—to look into the reason for its collapse four days after opening. At the present time I have no information to pass on. When I finish my investigation you'll be fully apprised of all the facts."

With surprising agility for a man that big, he was through the glass doors and gone before the crowd of news media could detain him with further questions.

"Underwipe and cut to commercial," Perry Worshak, the curly-haired young director, instructed.

"What does he think he's proving with all that secrecy?" Woody asked derisively. "You'd think he was chasing down a master spy."

Ray swiveled around in his chair. "You don't think the collapse of a school is important? It's a miracle that it happened at night and no one was injured."

"Well, sure it's important. I was just saying that this Hawke character better shape up. You can't treat the press like that and get away with it."

"What did you expect him to do, trot out all his suspicions so the guilty party will have time to cover up?" Pippa asked dryly.

"He could part with a *little* information," Woody snapped, angered at their joint disapproval. "He's so high and mighty he isn't even giving interviews."

Pippa looked at him skeptically. "How do you know that?"

"I phoned his advance people," Woody informed her smugly. "They said nothing doing until the investigation is wrapped up."

Wasn't it just like Woody to let his fingers do the walking? Pippa looked at him in disgust. "It's a wonder you didn't ask the man to write your story for you and mail it in."

For a moment it looked as though Woody were going to explode. Mastering his temper with difficulty, he smiled maliciously. "Running all over town wiggling your bottom in those tight jeans might make you look busy, but it doesn't get you any further than my methods —which are a lot more professional, I might add."

It was the sort of personal remark made expressly to get a rise out of her. Refusing to play his game, she pointed out the obvious. "You didn't get an interview."

"And neither could you."

"The story hasn't been assigned to me." Pippa shrugged.

A cunning gleam crept into his eyes. "If you got to talk to Hawke, it would *be* your story. But that's all right, kid. I'll let you off with that lame excuse."

Pippa gritted her teeth. A little of Woody went a long way, and she didn't have the disposition of a saint. In the interest of harmony in the newsroom, Pippa had been careful not to make waves, but enough was enough. It was time Woody was shown up for what he was.

She looked at him appraisingly. "And if I get the interview where you failed?"

"I have fifty bucks that says you can't."

"You're on," Pippa told him.

She was aware that Woody thought he had tricked her into the bet. It would add to her satisfaction when she collected. Actually Pippa had another reason for accepting the challenge. From the moment she saw Jeremy Hawke on the screen, he had fired her imagination. He was so competent, so assured. There was something exciting about the man. He was smashingly handsome of course, but it was more than that. There was a remote quality, a sense of fire under ice that was a challenge to any woman. She had to meet him if only to find out what color those light eyes were, Pippa told herself with secret amusement.

Perry stared at the small video screen in the top right-hand corner that showed what was going out over the air. It was marked with a red light. "Camera three, two-shot with Marilyn, now zoom to Wes," he said tersely. "Camera two, wide . . . and . . . roll credits. Okay, that's a wrap."

Everyone stood up, stretching after the tension of a live television show where anything could go wrong, and occasionally did. Under the cover of the ensuing chatter, Pippa slipped away.

Unlocking her car a few minutes later, she debated the advisability of changing clothes before going to the Beverly Wilshire where Jeremy Hawke was staying. The elegant hotel would frown on her jeans and denim jacket as Woody had, although attire in the newsroom was always casual.

The hotel would just have to withstand the shock, Pippa decided, wheeling expertly out of her parking space and starting down Sunset Boulevard. If Woody was right about Hawke's unavailability, the jeans were part of her alternate plan. So was the Greek fisherman's cap she pulled out of her jacket pocket. Before she got to the hotel, Pippa tucked her long hair into the cap, pulling the visor down to shade her face.

As she expected, the desk clerk haughtily informed her that Mr. Hawke was not seeing the press. No, she couldn't speak to him on the house phone. Yes, she could leave a message, although his manner indicated it wouldn't do any good.

Pippa accepted all this with a meekness that would have surprised those who knew her. Leaving the hotel, she went down the street to a florist where she chose an impressive arrangement of blooms in a ceramic pot. Approaching a different desk clerk she announced, "Flowers for Mr. Jeremy Hawke's suite."

As Pippa had half expected, the man said, "Leave them on the counter. I'll see that they're delivered."

She did as he said without argument, turning around and heading for the revolving door. Making a detour around a bellman wheeling a loaded baggage cart, Pippa

14

drifted to the right. Behind a large pillar she pulled off her cap, loosing the bright cloud of golden brown hair. She removed the denim jacket, revealing a red silk blouse with patch pockets over her small, curved breasts. A pair of large round sunglasses from her capacious shoulder bag completed the transformation.

Going up to the desk once more, Pippa took a pad of paper and a pen out of her purse. She rested it on the counter next to the floral arrangement while she concentrated on writing a note.

With the merest glance at her, the desk clerk tapped a bell. "Take these up to suite 809," he told the uniformed man who answered his summons.

Pippa put away her note pad and walked in the opposite direction, rounding a corner of the lobby to a corridor filled with elegant little shops. She looked in the windows for fifteen minutes before heading decisively for the bank of elevators, rummaging through her purse as though searching for her key.

Pippa was surprised to find that her heart was thumping in a most unaccustomed way as she waited for Jeremy Hawke to answer her knock. It wasn't like her to be nervous when she was on the trail of a story. What was there about this man that caused little ripples to travel up her spine?

Before she could figure it out, the door was flung open and he was there before her. Pippa drew in her breath involuntarily. Jeremy Hawke in the flesh seemed a little larger than life. She had seen how he towered over the others at the airport, so she shouldn't have been surprised, yet the small screen hadn't given the whole picture.

It couldn't convey the blatant masculinity radiating from that lean body, the sense of restless power held carefully in check. Pippa's reporter's eye took over as she made rapid mental notes. Jeremy Hawke, age . . . what? Thirty-six? Thirty-seven? No more than that. Dark brown hair, straight nose, high cheekbones that gave him

15

the subtle look of his namesake. Unusual light green eyes —so *that's* what color they were!

He was regarding her impatiently. "I'm on long distance. I'll be with you in a minute."

She was left to hover indecisively, watching the wide triangle of his back as he strode across the room. He had taken off his jacket, rolled up his sleeves, and removed his tie in preparation for work. Jeremy Hawke was obviously not a man to feel jet lag—or any other human emotion. That full lower lip hinted at sensuality, but the light green eyes had been cool and distant.

She closed the door behind her, moving unobtrusively into the suite.

"The others have been delayed—some foul-up with the luggage," he was saying impatiently into the phone. "I can't call Jennings until I have the report in front of me, so I'll have to get back to you." He put his forefinger briefly on the button, preparing to dial again, when he suddenly became aware of Pippa. "Oh, sorry. What can I do for you?"

"I'm from the florist," she announced.

He gave her a puzzled look. "So?"

"I'm afraid some flowers were delivered to you by mistake."

He glanced around the room, noticing the floral arrangement for the first time. It was still swathed in its protective green tissue, sitting on a coffee table in front of a pale blue brocade couch. "I guess that's it over there."

"Yes." Pippa made no move toward it.

In the act of turning away, he paused to frown at her. "Was there anything else?"

"No, I—I was just looking around. This is a beautiful suite."

An expression of annoyance crossed his lean face. "Yes, it's just dandy. And I have a lot of work to do in it, so if you'll take your flowers, Miss . . ."

"Alcott, Pippa Alcott," she supplied. Crossing her fingers that she wasn't overdoing it, Pippa gave him an ingenuous look. "You must be a very important man."

16

Jeremy Hawke's eyes narrowed. "What leads you to that conclusion?"

"This place." She waved her hand. "It must cost a fortune."

"Being rich isn't the same as being important."

Her even white teeth flashed in a grin. "A lot of people wouldn't agree with you."

"That's their problem," he said dryly as the phone rang. Scooping it up, he barked out a greeting. The tone of his voice changed drastically. "Well, hello! It's so good to hear your voice."

His wife? Pippa wondered before deciding against it. That sexy purr was the kind reserved for girlfriends, she thought cynically.

"I'm hoping to get up north, but it's too early to tell when," he continued. After a pause, his voice deepened. "You know I do."

Pippa moved out of his range of vision so she was free to study his quarter profile. She didn't need to see his eyes to know the coldness was gone. What would it be like to have this man in love with you? she wondered suddenly. To be cradled against that broad chest and feel those firm lips moving over yours with a sensual expertise? She made an involuntary little sound.

It was enough to attract his attention. With an exclamation of annoyance he told his caller, "I'll phone you later, Calla, when I can talk." There was distinct hostility in the face he turned to Pippa. "Don't you have to get back to work?"

"I wasn't trying to listen to your conversation," she assured him hastily.

"I don't see how you could have avoided it," he answered sarcastically. "Now, will you kindly leave so I can have a little privacy?"

Pippa inched toward the coffee table, thinking furiously. What excuse could she give for staying? The only one that occurred to her was pretty lame, but she didn't want to appear too bright anyway.

"Would you mind if I got a little water out of the

bathroom for those flowers? You're supposed to add some as soon as they're delivered. We always send them out kind of dry so they won't spill on the way."

His lifted eyebrow was sardonic. "Your precious posies over there have been in an air-conditioned room for a total of fifteen minutes. I doubt that they're about to die of thirst."

Pippa adopted a mournful expression. "You wouldn't want me to lose my job, would you?"

He gritted his teeth, controlling his irritation with an effort. "All right. Do your errand of mercy, only be quick about it."

Pippa purposely ignored the pitcher standing on the dresser along with an ice bucket. Filling a bathroom glass to the brim, she attempted to pour the contents into the tightly massed floral arrangement. Only part of it reached its target. The rest cascaded onto the coffee table as she had expected.

"Oh, look what I've done!" she squealed. "How could I have been so clumsy?"

"It must be a special gift," he muttered.

"Don't worry, I'll clean it up right away," she promised.

Whipping off her jacket, Pippa prepared to mop up the spill with it. The idea was that he wouldn't send her packing in wet clothes. Jeremy scotched that plan immediately.

His long fingers closed around her wrist in a firm grip. "Wouldn't a towel be more absorbent than denim?" he inquired sarcastically.

"I wouldn't think of using your towels."

"Get one," he ordered.

Pippa had no choice. On the way back she pondered alternate plans, which proved fruitless. Jeremy took the large bath towel from her, cleaning up the mess despite her protests. From the grim set of his face she could tell he had been pushed to the limit.

He picked up the bowl of flowers, thrusting them urgently at her. When Pippa's arms closed automatically around the bowl, it tipped. Her yelp was genuine this time as the cold water cascaded inside her blouse.

He swore pungently under his breath. "I hope you're satisfied."

"It was *your* fault!" Pippa pulled the clammy silk away from her wet skin, glaring indignantly up at him. "The least you could do is apologize."

"Take it off." Jeremy was decisive as always. "I'll call valet service and have it dried for you."

"What am I supposed to wear in the meantime?" she demanded. If this man thought she intended to sit and make casual conversation clad only in a bra and jeans, he was badly mistaken. The very thought made Pippa's temperature rise.

He disappeared into the bedroom, returning almost immediately with one of his shirts. "Here, put this on." His mouth formed a straight line of annoyance.

Pippa accepted it in equally grim silence, going into the bathroom to change.

Jeremy's shirt was laughably big on her, the shoulders drooping down her slender arms, and the cuffs completely hiding her hands. She rolled up the sleeves, tying the shirttails around her waist, since they were too long to tuck into her jeans.

When she reappeared in the living room, Jeremy started to laugh. It was his first relaxed emotion of the day. "You look like the loser in a grab-bag contest."

The derision of this handsome, sophisticated man struck a nerve. "I'm glad you find *something* amusing, Mr. Hawke."

His mirth died suddenly. "How very interesting." Jeremy's voice was dangerously soft. "You know exactly who I am."

Pippa's blue eyes darkened with dismay. What on earth was the matter with her? She hadn't made a stupid mistake like that since she was a cub reporter. There was nothing she could do to retrieve the situation either; Jeremy Hawke was too astute a man. Well, there was nothing to do but take her leave gracefully—or at least with as much aplomb as she could manage.

"It just occurred to me that I saw your picture in the paper last night," she said, grabbing her jacket and backing away.

His hand shot out, fastening around her wrist. "Not so fast. You have a few questions to answer first."

His fingers were like a handcuff. "Please, Mr. Hawke, I —I really have to get back to work."

"Oh, yes, the flowers that were delivered by mistake," he said mockingly. "You didn't seem in any great hurry up till now."

Pippa tried to ignore the apprehension that chilled her as he drew her closer, menacing her with the power of that lithe body. "If I don't leave now, I might lose my job."

"And if you stay, you might get a bonus." His eyes were hard as he surveyed her anxious face. "Who are you, Pippa Alcott?"

"I . . . that's really my name."

"I have no doubt of that. What I should have asked was, what newspaper do you work for?"

"I don't work for any paper." It was a relief to be able to tell the truth for once.

He pulled her slightly toward him. "We can do this the easy way, or the hard way. It's up to you."

Pippa wasn't easily intimidated. She had interviewed people from every walk of life without ever encountering anyone like Jeremy Hawke. What form would his retribution take? The only course open to her was to stall for time.

"I don't know what you're talking about," she murmured.

"Then let me clarify it. I can call the police and have you arrested on suspicion of just about anything. You got into my suite under false pretenses."

They both knew the charge would never stick, but Pippa didn't want to go through the hassle. Ray wouldn't appreciate having to go to bat for her. She had a sudden inspiration. Lowering her lashes, Pippa slipped back into her little girl act.

"All right, Mr. Hawke, I'll tell you the truth."

"That would be refreshing," he said dryly.

"It's true the flowers weren't delivered to you by mistake. I sent them so I'd have an excuse to get in here."

"Now tell me something I *don't* know."

She caught her lip fetchingly between small white teeth, looking up at him appealingly. "It was all just a joke. A bunch of us were sitting around the sorority house watching the news. We saw you get off the plane, and everyone said how handsome you were, and how we'd love to meet you. One thing led to another . . . you know how it is."

"No, I don't. Suppose you tell me." His blank expression wasn't reassuring.

"Well, I said it shouldn't be that difficult to get in to see you. The other girls said it would be impossible, so it became sort of a challenge. After they dared me, I couldn't very well back down." Pippa couldn't manage any tears, but she dropped her eyelashes and gave a little sniffle. "I thought you might be a little angry, but I didn't know you'd threaten to call the police."

When he tipped her chin up with a long forefinger, Pippa refused to look at him, staring at his belt buckle instead. She held her breath under his searching gaze.

"Didn't your mother ever tell you about the trouble you can get into going to a man's hotel room?"

She let out her breath at his teasing tone. "I'm sorry, Mr. Hawke, truly I am."

"Why don't you make that Jeremy?"

She looked up then—and was struck dumb at his potent charm. If Jeremy Hawke had been attractive in anger, he was positively dazzling with a warm smile on his tan face.

"Come sit down and tell me about yourself," he said, leading her over to the couch.

"I've taken up enough of your time." Pippa was torn between wanting to leave before he discovered her deception and hating to break the tenuous contact between them.

"Let me worry about that," he said. "I should really be the one to apologize, but I've been hounded beyond endurance by reporters. They've done everything, including hiding under my bed." He gave her a wide grin. "You've no idea how that inhibits one's sex life."

"I guess it's their job." Pippa smoothed her jean-clad knee carefully. "Everything you do is news."

"Not *everything*. What possible interest can it be to the public to know what I eat for breakfast, or how many times I date the same woman?"

"It's called human interest." Pippa hurried to cover her inadvertent slip. "I mean, we all like to read about the little inside details of famous people's lives."

"I'm not famous." He sighed. "Just a hard-working stiff trying to clean up a dirty mess."

"Then you think there definitely was collusion involved in awarding that contract for Evergreen Elementary?"

Jeremy's expression cooled perceptibly. "You put that very professionally."

Pippa's heart started to thump. She would simply have to be more careful. Giving him an eager look she said, "Did I? I'm so happy to hear that. I'm a journalism major. Someday I hope to be one of those big-time reporters you hate so much."

He smiled wryly. "With your inventiveness, I'd say you're going to make it."

As though thinking of it for the first time, Pippa said, "Would you give me an interview? It would practically assure me a place on the campus paper."

Jeremy shook his head. "Come around at the end of the investigation. I'll be giving a briefing to all the media at the same time."

A sixth sense warned her not to push the point. She had already gotten further than all the other reporters. If she played it cool, she might wind up with a scoop.

"What school do you go to, Pippa?"

"U.C.L.A." She really had graduated from there, although it was almost five years ago.

"Good school." He nodded. "Fine football team too."

"Where did you go to college?" Pippa asked, although she already knew the answer.

"Stanford." His smile was rueful. "When you were still in diapers."

It was aggravating, yet essential, that he think of her as a girl instead of as a woman. In spite of that, Pippa tried to disparage the difference in their ages. "You make me sound so juvenile. I'm really quite mature."

There was laughter in the green eyes that swept her curved body. "So I've noticed."

Pippa felt her cheeks growing warm, another unusual reaction he provoked. "I didn't mean *that.*"

"How old are you, Pippa? Nineteen? Twenty?"

"Somewhere around there," she answered evasively.

Jeremy chuckled. "Hang in there, honey. One day you'll be fudging about your age in the other direction."

"Is that what the woman you were talking to on the phone does?" she asked coolly.

"Calla? What interest would you have in her?"

Pippa shrugged. "I was just wondering what kind of woman you're attracted to."

He laughed lightly. "You've just said the operative word—woman. I don't fool around with little girls."

She raised her chin pugnaciously. "You just like to threaten them with the police."

"You don't look cowed exactly," he commented dryly.

"Is that the way you like your women, submissive?"

"As a matter of fact, no. I like spirit—in a man *or* a woman."

This man was proving to be a worthy opponent. Pippa regarded him appraisingly. "I think we're going to get along just fine."

His face held a mixture of amusement and disbelief. "Starting when?" he drawled.

It was the opening she was looking for. "How about

tonight? I'll go home and change, and we can go out to dinner."

Jeremy's newfound goodwill was cooling rapidly. "Exactly what else did that bet with your sorority sisters include?"

"Nothing," she assured him hastily. "That wasn't part of it. It was my own idea. I want to get to know you better."

He looked faintly dazed. "I've heard about the sexual revolution, but I didn't realize how extensive it is. In my day, the man made the dates."

"But you wouldn't have asked me," Pippa pointed out.

"That's true." He smiled. "I can't quarrel with that logic."

"So, is it a date?"

"It most certainly is not," he stated firmly. As she opened her mouth to launch a flood of arguments, Jeremy said, "For one thing, I had dinner on the plane. It's three hours later for me."

"Oh." Pippa was only momentarily thrown for a loss. "How about tomorrow then? I'll pick you up in the morning and give you the grand tour."

He was silent for a long moment, staring at her consideringly. "I must admit to being baffled by you, Pippa, and that's a more amazing admission than you realize. Are you merely an impudent child—or a woman I should be very wary of?"

There was a quality to his low voice that made a shiver run up her spine. Pippa forced herself to appear unruffled. "How could I pose any threat to you?"

"Very easily." Something flared briefly in his eyes, then was gone as though a curtain dropped. "I came here on business, not pleasure."

She chose to misunderstand his clipped statement. "You're entitled to some leisure time, especially since you're an unpaid consultant."

He grinned suddenly. "Maybe if I work hard, they'll give me a salaried job."

They both knew that was a joke. Pippa regarded him

curiously. "I know the money doesn't mean anything to you, but there are other considerations. Why would you chuck the whole thing to go to Washington and be just a cog in the machinery? You're head of an important business of your own here in California."

"You aren't the first person who has asked that." His expression was wry. "Most of them don't understand even after I've explained it."

"Try me."

Jeremy stared out the window, although darkness had fallen, and even the twinkling lights were obscured by the sheer white curtains under the brocade drapes.

"One reason is that I think everyone should put back at least part of what they take out of life," he answered slowly. "I've had a remarkably cushioned existence. In a way, donating some time to the government is like knocking on wood." He smiled suddenly, a charming smile that lit up his strong face. "Another, less noble reason is that I wanted to get out of the sterile environment of facts and figures for a while, and into the world of people. You tend to feel a little isolated when everything you read is composed of little dots."

"At least they tell you the truth. Won't this investigation be difficult for you?"

"You mean because everyone is covering up?"

"Are they?" Pippa asked carefully.

Jeremy's eyes narrowed as he failed to take the bait. "You're remarkably good at this sort of thing. I predict a brilliant future for you as a reporter."

"You haven't answered my question."

"Did you expect me to?"

She shrugged. "Why not? It was academic anyway. You wouldn't be here unless there was some evidence of wrongdoing."

"Haven't you ever heard of a routine investigation?"

Pippa looked around the luxurious suite. "If this is just routine, I'm going to complain about how my tax dollars are being spent."

He chuckled. "You're too young to have paid in

enough to cover room service. How old are you, Pippa? You still haven't told me."

"That isn't a question you ask a woman."

"It's only one of the things I want to know." He stared at her searchingly. "You intrigue me, Pippa. Tell me about yourself."

"After you've finished with *your* story," she evaded.

"What more is there to tell?"

"A million things; you've merely scratched the surface."

He sighed. "Don't tell me you're like all the others, fascinated by what I have for breakfast?"

"No, and I'm not going to hide under your bed either."

Jeremy's voice deepened to a husky pitch. "That's good. I'm finding, much to my surprise, that I'd rather have you in it."

The glow in his eyes lit an answering warmth in the pit of her stomach. Pippa tried to ignore it. "What happened to all your good resolutions about business before pleasure?"

"You convinced me that I need a little recreation. Weren't you offering to help me relax?" he teased.

"You could accomplish that with a glass of warm milk," she informed him tartly. "I don't enjoy being equated with a sleeping pill."

"I was never more wide awake," he assured her, tracing the shape of her cheek with a long forefinger.

The essentially innocent gesture was unbearably sensuous. Pippa caught her breath. "I think I'd better be leaving."

"You're probably right," he answered almost absently, his eyes on her full mouth.

Pippa was powerless to move. Every instinct told her to head for the door, but she was caught in the web of his magnetism, drawn toward Jeremy Hawke by a force as old as nature. She tried to shake off the feeling. "It—it was nice meeting you."

"You too," he murmured without taking his eyes from hers.

Jeremy's dark head bent toward her bright one, almost in slow motion. His mouth covered hers gently at first, savoring its sweetness. Pippa drew a sharp breath, putting her hands against his chest. He didn't try to overpower her. Instead, his tongue gently outlined the shape of her lips, probing delicately with a sensual suggestion. When she turned her head, his warm mouth slid along her cheek, exploring the inner contours of her ear.

Pippa might have been able to withstand an aggressive attack, but this slow seduction set up a clamor in her veins that refused to be denied. He had stripped away her defenses so subtly that she wasn't even aware of it. Deaf to everything but the dictates of her body, she sighed softly, putting her arms around his neck and running slim fingers through his crisp hair.

With a low growl of satisfaction his arms closed around her, drawing Pippa into an embrace that acquainted her with every hard muscle in that lean, male body. His kiss deepened into a promise of delight as his hands caressed the smooth skin of her back, under the hiked-up shirt.

She returned his kiss with an abandon completely foreign to her until now, lost in the magic of a man she seemed to have been waiting for all her life. Every one of her senses was alive to the electrifying touch of his hands, his lips, his body. Pippa was floating in a world so fraught with sensation that she felt bereft when Jeremy raised his head. It took a long moment before she realized there was a repeated knocking at the door.

"Oh, no!" Jeremy groaned. "How could I have let a thing like this happen?"

"Are you in there, Jeremy?" a male voice called.

Another voice speculated, "Maybe he's in the shower. Should I go down and get another key?"

Pippa's dazed eyes met Jeremy's as he helped her to her feet.

"It's all right, honey." He smoothed her hair tenderly. "Don't look so stricken."

Reality was starting to take over. She clutched his arm.

"You can't let them in! My clothes . . . your shirt . . ." She could just imagine what conclusions those men, whoever they were, would draw!

"Go into my bedroom," Jeremy said in a low voice. "There's a door leading out to the corridor. Don't worry, they won't come in there." He led her into the next room, closing the door firmly.

Pippa waited until she heard voices in the living room before slipping out noiselessly. Her eyes were feverishly bright as she ran down the hall to the elevator, her one thought being to escape without notice.

It was only when she was in her car headed down Wilshire Boulevard that Pippa began to berate herself. How could she have allowed this to happen? Her indictment unconsciously echoed Jeremy's. She had come here to stalk *him*—and turned into prey herself. There was absolutely no excuse for it. It wasn't as though she were the young innocent he thought her. She was usually more than a match for any man. What black magic had he practiced on her?

Pippa refused to admit that Jeremy had tried to send her on her way before things got that far. It was galling enough to remember her completely abandoned reaction to his experienced lovemaking. She was certainly no match for him in that department!

The whole evening had been a complete disaster. She didn't even have a story to show for it. Without knowing it, Jeremy Hawke had more than gotten his own back against the dreaded reporters he detested so much.

CHAPTER TWO

Pippa's small apartment in Westwood felt like a haven. Shedding her clothes in the bathroom, she turned the shower to a needle spray, letting it scourge her delicate skin. She soaped her body and scrubbed her face, trying to rid herself of every vestige of Jeremy Hawke's caresses. If only she could get him out of her mind that easily. What an opinion he must have of her—"pushover" would be about the kindest way of putting it. How could she convince him that such a thing had never happened before? The answer was simple—she couldn't.

Pippa turned off the shower and stepped out, wrapping herself in a large bath towel. The best thing would be to chalk it up to experience and see that it never happened again. It was easy to tell herself to put him completely out of her mind. In actual practice it was impossible.

After putting on a robe Pippa wandered into the kitchen, realizing that she hadn't had any dinner. When everything in the refrigerator seemed to make her faintly ill, she gave up and climbed into bed with a book. For almost an hour she turned the pages diligently without having any idea of what she had read. When the phone rang, it was a welcome relief.

"I'm sorry to call so late, Pippa, but I've been trying all evening and you weren't home."

It was Gloria Cullen, the newest addition to the newsroom team. She was small, dark, vivacious, and filled with enthusiasm for her job. She and Pippa had hit it off immediately, partly because they were about the same age, and partly due to Gloria's obvious hero worship. It would be hard not to like someone who regarded you as the best newswriter in the West.

"That's okay, I was just reading," Pippa assured her. "What's up, Gloria?"

"I have to talk to you. Can I come over?"

"Now?" Pippa glanced at the clock. It was after eleven.

"I know it's late, but I can't face another day in the newsroom without getting some advice." Gloria sounded really anguished.

"Well, sure, if it's that important," Pippa said slowly.

She got up and lit the lights in the living room, then put on a pot of coffee. What could be troubling Gloria that greatly? Pippa hoped it wasn't anything to do with her marriage. Scott Cullen was a delight, always ready with a compliment and a cheerful smile. He was in his last year at medical school, and Pippa had a feeling that they were often strapped for money. It would be a shame if it were causing dissension in their marriage. That was often the case though when the woman was the bread-winner, even if only temporarily.

The young couple lived near her, so Pippa didn't have long to wait for the answer. Gloria rang the bell a scant ten minutes later.

She started to apologize as soon as she came in. "You're an angel to let me barge in on you like this. I know it's a real imposition."

"Hey, come on, no problem. Would you like some coffee? I just made a fresh pot."

"I'd love some." Gloria followed her into the kitchen.

Pippa filled two cups, carrying them to the round breakfast table. "How is Scott?" she asked warily.

"Sound asleep I hope."

"He . . . uh . . . he's at home then?" Pippa picked her way carefully.

"Yes, he's been cramming for exams every night this week. About ten o'clock he was so beat that he set the alarm for six, and fell into bed. I don't think there's any chance that he'll wake up and find I've gone out."

"Why would he mind if you came over here?"

"He wouldn't. It's just that I—" Gloria's hand was shaking so badly she had to set her coffee cup down. "Oh, Pip, everything is such a mess. I love my job at the station; I don't want to lose it."

"Why would you even think of a thing like that?" Pippa exclaimed.

Gloria had been at KCTV only a little over a month, but she was well liked and a willing worker. She took criticism well, was eager to learn, and she never complained about the stories assigned to her.

"I know I'm not in your class," Gloria said earnestly. "But—"

"Nonsense!" Pippa didn't let her finish. "I just have more experience; I've been at it longer. This is your first TV job."

"I hope it isn't my last," Gloria said somberly.

"As far as I know, Ray is completely satisfied with your work. What happened to put you in such a state?"

Gloria bent her head over her cup. "It's Woody," she said in a low voice.

Pippa made a sound of annoyance. "Is *that* all? You shouldn't let that creep bother you! His high school mentality thinks it's funny to haze every newcomer."

"I wish that's all it was. Haven't you noticed the way he picks apart every word I write? Or the disparaging little comments he makes in front of Hal during the briefing meetings?"

"When you get to know him better, you'll discover that the only person Woody has a good word to say about is himself," Pippa said dryly. "He isn't singling you out, he's just doing what comes naturally. If you don't show it's getting to you, he'll stop after a while."

Gloria shook her head. "You don't know the whole

story." She stared down at her cup. "I knew Woody before I came to KCTV."

Pippa was startled. Surely that didn't mean what it sounded like. She found it hard to visualize Gloria having anything to do with a wimp like Woody. "It's funny that neither of you mentioned it. I can see why you'd want to take back your introduction to *him*," she said slowly. "But it isn't like Woody to be that reticent."

"He didn't recognize me when I first started to work. It was a long time ago, and I hoped he'd forgotten about me."

"Maybe you'd better start at the beginning," Pippa said gently.

Gloria's shoulders sagged. "It all happened three years ago in Sacramento—that's where I grew up. I was just out of college, an eager would-be writer. The annual writer's conference there is one of the better ones, so I thought I could pick up some valuable tips on how to break into the field. You get to meet editors and agents who tell you what they're looking for. There are also seminars conducted by professionals from every phase of the industry."

"I've never been to one, but I understand you can gain valuable experience."

"In more ways than one." Gloria's smile was wry. "Woody was the guest lecturer on television newswriting."

Pippa nodded. She had recently found out that he attended every year. It came up in conversation because the conference was nearing again. "It must be a terrific ego trip for Woody. Under any other circumstances he wouldn't give a beginner the time of day."

"His seminars were always full," Gloria acknowledged. "That's why I was so excited when he seemed to single me out."

"Oh, no!" Pippa groaned.

"I was very young, and he was an important older man," Gloria said defensively. "I couldn't believe it was a personal interest. After all, what would he want with a small-town girl when he must know all kinds of interesting women?"

Pippa looked at her friend's delicate flowerlike face. She must have been an enchanting youngster. At that moment her dislike of Woody turned to loathing. "So he asked you for a date and you found out."

"No, it wasn't like that. I might have caught on if he had. I was young, but I wasn't stupid." A flash of humor lit her strained face. "On the last day of the conference he told me my work had great promise and he'd like to give me some pointers. Unfortunately there wasn't time in the seminars, but maybe he could spare half an hour afterward. He suggested I go to the bar in his hotel, and if he could break away, he'd meet me there. He even asked me to forgive him if he didn't make it."

"Very smooth," Pippa commented reluctantly.

"You can see how I was thrown off the track. I gathered together all the best samples of my writing and got there way ahead of time. When Woody showed up, I was thrilled at how kind he was being to a little nobody. He even ordered champagne."

"On the expense account—which is the only way he ever picks up a check. And *then* he pads the bill," Pippa said dryly. Woody's expenses accounted for his most creative writing. They were a constant source of battles with the station manager.

"I was so nervous I gulped down the first glass like water, but he went out of his way to put me at ease. He told me some funny stories about his early days, and then he read the articles I'd brought. He also filled my glass every time it was empty."

Pippa's lip curled contemptuously. "The perfect host."

"I can't honestly blame him for getting me drunk; that was my own stupidity. You know how it is, though, when someone reads your material right in front of you. Or maybe you don't, because you're a professional. But I was only a novice, remember. I sat there examining his expression, trying to tell if I was wasting his time. Did I

33

really have talent, or was I just kidding myself? And I kept emptying my glass."

"What words of wisdom did he finally impart?"

"He showed me how to tighten up one article and pointed out where another was structured wrong. Then he said there were some scripts in his room from an actual news show. By studying them I'd not only learn the format, but all the jargon as well. Woody said it was important to present your work in a professional manner."

"It didn't occur to you to ask him to bring them down to the bar?"

"I didn't have a chance. He looked at his watch and said he didn't realize it was so late. He had an appointment with an editor. Besides, I couldn't ask for any more favors after he'd done so much for me."

"Good old heart-of-gold Woody. So of course you went up to his room with him."

"Floated up would be a better description. Everything seemed to be spinning around like an out-of-control merry-go-round. Woody said I looked pale and I'd better lie down on the bed for a while." Gloria swirled the cooling coffee around in her cup. "I honestly don't remember very much more. Luckily, I realized what was going on before anything serious happened . . . but the whole scene was just so awful, Pippa. It's been years and I still can't think about it without feeling sick to my stomach."

"You poor kid." Pippa went to turn on the heat under the coffee, giving Gloria a chance to compose herself.

"I got out of there and I've never mentioned it to a soul since."

"I can understand." Pippa nodded. "But why would you come to work at KCTV? Surely you must have known Woody was still on the staff?"

"It was foolish, I suppose, but it was my first big break. I couldn't bear to pass it up. My credentials from a little suburban paper in Sacramento didn't impress anyone in Los Angeles. I had applications in at every newspaper, radio, and TV station, but all I ever got were promises.

34

Then after Scott and I were married a year ago, I didn't have the luxury of time. We needed my salary. I'm not complaining, though. Being married to Scott is the most wonderful thing that ever happened to me."

Pippa looked at the love shining out of her friend's eyes. "You don't have to tell me that," she said fondly.

"I was doing secretarial work when I heard about the job at KCTV. Naturally I knew about Woody, but it was so long ago. Anyway, under the circumstances I didn't think there was a chance he'd remember me," she said with bitter self-mockery.

"But he did?"

"Not at first. He kept staring at me as though wondering whether he'd ever seen me before, or if I just looked like someone he knew. He asked a lot of questions, too, which I kind of laughed off. Then one day in the newsroom some of the fellows were kidding him about his annual trek to beautiful downtown Sacramento. I could almost see the wheels turn as everything clicked into place."

"Don't tell me even Woody would have the gall to try to renew old acquaintances!"

Gloria raised one eyebrow. "You keep telling me you know him. He not only had the gall, he hinted, not too delicately, that if I wasn't . . . friendly the story might get around. He even threatened to tell Scott." Gloria looked down at her coffee cup. "Even though nothing really happened, God only knows what Woody's version of the evening would sound like."

"You realize it was a bluff, don't you?" Pippa asked angrily. "Something like that wouldn't put *him* in a very good light."

"I was too upset to think straight at the time—upset and revolted. When I told him how I felt about him, he changed tactics. I didn't think anybody could be as cruel and rotten as that man!" Gloria cried passionately. "He's going to get me fired!"

"Calm down." Pippa soothed her friend. "Woody has nothing to do with hiring or firing."

"Not directly, but that isn't his way anyhow," Gloria said bitterly. "He's started a campaign to undermine me. In briefing sessions he says things like, 'Why don't you let Gloria have that story? It's in the B segment near the end of the show; it won't matter what she does to it.' He's also turning the anchors against me. Remember that story on the abandoned baby found in a movie theater? A story of mine that *Woody* rewrote, incidentally! When Wes complained about it, Woody said he'd told me it was lousy, but I insisted that it go on exactly as I wrote it. Wes was fit to be tied."

Wesley Taylor, the anchorman, was more than a little temperamental. Pippa could imagine what his reaction would be to an answer like that. The trouble was, it was a no-win situation. There was only Gloria's word against Woody's, and he was always careful to stay on cordial terms with the anchorpeople, who had been known to get a writer fired.

"I guess you could discuss it with Ray," Pippa said reluctantly, knowing that wasn't the best advice. Management was reluctant to get into personal squabbles. Presumably they were all adult enough to handle their own differences.

Watching the play of emotions over Pippa's expressive face, Gloria smiled grimly. "Wouldn't Woody enjoy *that?* It would give him an opportunity to expand on his favorite theme—the emotional inferiority of women."

She was right of course. As usual, Woody had covered all bases. "There must be some way to stop him," Pippa exclaimed angrily. "Nobody can keep getting away with the foul things he pulls."

Gloria sighed. "I suppose he'll stub his toe one day. I just hope it isn't too late to do me any good."

"Hang in there; I'll think of something." It wasn't an idle promise. Pippa was fed up with Woody Phelan. The time had come for some bare knuckle fighting.

"I hope so." Gloria didn't sound convinced. A lot of the tension was gone, though, as she pushed back her chair. "Thanks for listening to me anyway. I feel better just telling someone about it. And now I should be starting back."

Pippa walked her to the door. "Try not to let Woody see he's getting to you. That will spoil part of his fun to begin with." She grinned suddenly. "And if you could manage a secret little smile when you pass his desk, it might worry him a bit. Woody's so tricky, he figures everyone else is up to something too."

"I'll try anything." Gloria hugged Pippa impulsively. "Thanks, friend, it's good to have you on my side."

After she left, Pippa rinsed out the cups, thinking furiously. There had to be a way to help Gloria; it was just a question of finding it. The sordid story crystallized her determination. Why were all men so rotten? she wondered angrily. They regarded every woman as a challenge. Which brought Jeremy Hawke inevitably to mind.

Gloria's troubles had obliterated all thoughts of him for a blessed period. Now he was back in full force. Pippa didn't welcome the memory of that darkly handsome face and compelling male body. Mixed in with the embarrassment and lack of self-respect was an inexplicable, yet aching sense of loss.

A jangling noise finally succeeded in waking Pippa the next morning. At first she buried her nose in the pillow until all that was visible was a cloud of golden brown hair. When the sound refused to go away, she opened drowsy eyes. The bedside clock said it was almost seven thirty, time to get up. But it wasn't the alarm that woke her, it was the telephone.

The deep male voice that greeted her drove away all lethargy. "I hope I'm not calling too early," Jeremy Hawke said.

"No, I—I'm awake." She was now!

"I wanted to phone last night, but it was after one o'clock when I finished getting a briefing from my aides." He was a lot more alert than Pippa on even less sleep.

"What did you want?" she asked abruptly.

"To see if you were all right."

37

"Of course I am. Why wouldn't I be?"

"I was afraid you might be upset."

If he only knew! Pippa pulled the covers up to her chin as though Jeremy could see her slender body in the wispy nightgown. "It wasn't my finest hour. Do you have any idea what it feels like to slip out of a man's hotel room like a . . . well, you know."

"I thought it would be less embarrassing for you."

"It would have been less embarrassing if you hadn't brought it up again," she answered bitterly.

"I wanted to apologize," he said simply.

Suddenly Pippa's anger dissolved. What an extraordinarily kind man he was. Most men would have considered her merely the one who got away. There was a catch in her voice as she said, "You didn't have to do that. I could have stopped you. What happened was as much my fault as yours."

"No, it wasn't. I'm a mature man, I should have exercised better control. But learn by experience, Pippa. You're a beautiful girl; men will always try to take advantage of you."

She couldn't tell him that she had always passed the test with flying colors before. "Well, nothing happened anyway," she said lamely.

"Thank God!"

The heartfelt gratitude in his voice irritated her. "That isn't very flattering," she said stiffly.

He made a low sound of annoyance. "What am I going to do with you? Didn't you hear a word I said?"

"Of course I did, but—"

"Let me put it more bluntly. If my men hadn't showed up when they did, you might easily have found yourself in bed with a total stranger. I didn't get to know you very well, Pippa, but I think that would have caused you a great deal of misery. Am I right?"

"Yes," she murmured, her cheeks very pink.

"Good. Then you realize why I said I was glad."

"I only meant that—" She took a deep breath. "Weren't you even a *little* bit sorry?"

Jeremy started to laugh. "Do you want to be reassured that you're desirable? All right, I'll oblige. How's this? Although I managed to put you out of my mind for a time while the men were briefing me on the situation here, when I got into bed you returned in living color. I wanted you there next to me with that golden brown hair drifting over my bare chest."

"Jeremy, I—"

"Be quiet. You asked for this. I wanted to undress you very slowly, kissing every inch of satin skin as I got you out of those ridiculous jeans and into my arms. I could almost hear you calling my name as I discovered what pleased you most. I wanted to prolong your delight until you begged me to make love to you. Then I dreamed of losing myself in your beautiful body." His voice was a sensuous purr. "Does that answer your question?"

Pippa was having trouble breathing. "You—you're making fun of me."

"Far from it, my dear. I'm making love to you. The only way that's safe—over the telephone," he said dryly.

"Anyone would think you're afraid of me," she protested.

"And anyone would be right."

"That isn't fair! What happened was just a crazy, once in a lifetime set of circumstances."

"Maybe." He sounded skeptical. "At any rate, you made an impression that's going to stay with me for a long time."

There was a note of finality in his voice. Jeremy had made his apology, and he was going out of her life. Last night Pippa would have welcomed the idea, wanting only to put the whole wretched incident out of her mind. So why did the thought of never seeing him again send her into a panic? She didn't have time to examine her feelings —in another second he would be gone.

"I don't want you to remember me like that, Jeremy! Couldn't you give me another chance?"

"To do what?" He sounded astonished.

"To prove to you that I'm not a flaky college kid out for a quick thrill."

"I don't think that, honey."

"Then you'll let me show you around the way you promised before . . . well, you know."

"Did I do that? You have me so baffled, Pippa, that I'm not quite sure what went on."

"Well, maybe you didn't exactly promise, but you were considering it." She rushed on before he could comment. "I could pick you up at your hotel in an hour and we—"

"Hold it!" he chuckled. "I'm here to conduct an investigation, remember? I haven't even started work yet."

Pippa was undaunted. "How about Saturday then? You can't work on weekends. All the government offices are closed, private industry too."

"I know I'm being old-fashioned," he said dryly, "but just once would you allow *me* to be the one to make the date?"

"Certainly, Jeremy," Pippa answered demurely. "I'd be delighted to accept your invitation for Saturday afternoon. There, is that better?"

He laughed unwillingly. "Listen to me, my outrageous little friend. I wouldn't get within twenty city blocks of you."

"Oh, for heaven's sake, Jeremy! What could possibly happen out in public in broad daylight?"

"That's something I don't intend to find out."

"Do you have a date with Miss Calla Lily?" Pippa demanded. "Is that it?"

"Interesting that you should call her that," he reflected, without replying directly. "I never thought about it before, but that's a good description of her."

A mental image arose of a cool beauty who would remain unruffled in any situation. Pippa felt a pang, remembering how she had flunked the test. "I suppose *I* remind you of poison ivy," she said acidly to cover the hurt that implied.

There was amusement in his voice. "No, you're more

like a Venus's-flytrap—prettier, yet structured along the same lines."

"How can I convince you that all I want from you is—" The rush of words stopped as Pippa realized with horror that she had almost revealed her true purpose—an interview. "I just want us to be friends," she finished carefully.

"I'd be very proud to consider myself your friend," Jeremy said quietly.

"I was only going to take you to Olvera Street for lunch," she continued plaintively. "That's where Los Angeles began, back in the days when it was a little Spanish pueblo. I thought you'd enjoy seeing it."

"I'm sure I would. I—it's just that I don't think it's a good idea."

Sensing a weakening, Pippa turned persuasive. "I'll get you back in plenty of time for your date." She was careful not to use her derogatory name for his girlfriend.

"If you're referring to Calla, we don't have a date." Pippa's joy was tempered as he added, "She lives in San Francisco. I don't expect to see her until this is all over—the investigation I mean."

"Then there's no problem. I'll give you a quick orientation tour, and you can amaze your colleagues with how well you did your homework."

"Why would you want to give up a Saturday to be with me?" he temporized.

"I have nothing better to do," she answered carelessly.

He wasn't buying. "Try again."

The terse reply warned Pippa that one false move on her part would allow Jeremy to slip off the hook. "It isn't any of the things you're thinking. If you'd made a bad impression on someone, wouldn't you want to correct it?" She had a sudden thought. "As a matter of fact, wouldn't you rather remember a pleasantly innocent afternoon with me than last night's fiasco?"

"You might be right at that," he said slowly.

Pippa let out the breath she had been holding unconsciously. "Is it a deal then?"

41

He sighed. "Against every ounce of better judgment I possess—it's a deal."

"Oh, thank you, Jeremy! We'll have such fun. I'll show you a terrific time."

"Hold it right there! Before I see you again we're going to set down some ground rules. This woman's liberation thing is all right for boys—the ones who grew up with it. I happen to be a man who is used to acting like one. This role reversal has been known to cause impotence." He sounded downright plaintive.

Pippa bubbled over with laughter. "What are you worried about? That means I won't constitute any danger."

"If it's all the same to you, I'd like to exercise my own constraint."

"The occasion won't arise," she promised. "It's going to be a completely non-threatening afternoon. I'll pick you up at twelve and we—"

"Correction, my dear. I'll pick *you* up, *I'll* do the driving, and *I* pay for the lunch. Is that clear?"

"How about two out of three?"

"What do you mean?"

"You don't know the city, so you're apt to get lost trying to find my apartment. We'll take my car, but you can drive," she added hastily.

"I suppose that makes sense," he answered reluctantly. "Which isn't necessarily the case. You could convince a polar bear to turn vegetarian."

Before he could have second thoughts, Pippa said hurriedly, "I'll be at the motor entrance of the hotel at noon on Saturday. Look for a white Mustang." She hung up without waiting for his reply.

While she was rushing around the small apartment getting dressed, Pippa felt as though she were filled with helium. What a difference Jeremy's phone call had made. Last night she had been sunk into the depths; now suddenly everything was all right. Surely in the relaxed intimacy of an afternoon alone with Jeremy she could talk him into an interview.

Pippa assured herself it was her failure that had been

bothering her as much as last night's debacle. If the thought of spending time alone with such a fascinating man wasn't exactly distasteful, well, what was wrong with enjoying your work?

Things were slow at the newsroom for once. The winter storms and flooding had subsided, the criminal element of the city seemed to be taking a break—at least where newsworthy crimes were concerned—and even the President hadn't done anything controversial lately.

At the meeting that morning Ray said, "We'll have to fill in tonight with a lot of human interest stuff. I pulled these off the City News Service." He referred to the papers in his hand. "We'll give some footage to that off-beat dog show in Griffith Park—the one to pick the ugliest mutt. And this might be a good time to do an in-depth segment on real estate costs throughout the country. Lean on the angle that California is up there with the highest in the nation."

There was a marked lack of enthusiasm from the seasoned reporters lounging around the room. "How about the investigation on Evergreen Elementary?" Woody reminded the producer. "That's a big one."

"The trouble is, Hawke isn't giving any interviews, and neither are the people around him. We'll give it a mention, of course, but there's only so much mileage you can get out of stock shots of the school and reruns of him saying, 'No comment.' "

"Why don't you put Pippa on it?" Woody asked. "She bet me that she could get an interview."

When Ray raised an eyebrow in her direction Pippa said, "I'm working on it."

Woody's smile was unpleasant. "Which means you have the same chance as the rest of us—little and none."

"I wouldn't say that. I have an appointment with Mr. Hawke on Saturday." Pippa thoroughly enjoyed the dumbfounded look that crossed Woody's face.

His mouth actually fell open before he got control of

himself. "Congratulations. It seems I underestimated that wiggle of yours," he said mockingly.

"I've never had that trouble, Woody," Pippa commented dryly. "It's impossible to underestimate *you.*"

Ray stepped in deftly. "That's great, Pippa. How did you manage it?"

"Yes, tell all of us how the intrepid girl reporter succeeded where everyone else failed," Woody baited her.

She surveyed him coolly. "If you don't know by now how to get an interview, I'm afraid you're in the wrong business." Turning to Ray, she said, "I can't be sure how much will come of it. He's pretty cagey. Everything so far has been off the record, but at least it's a foot in the door."

"That's right. Just stay with it," Ray encouraged her.

After the stories had been assigned, the reporters headed for their desks and telephones. All except Woody. He trailed after Pippa, folding his arms and leaning against her desk as though he had nothing to do. "Tell me the truth, how did you get an appointment with Hawke?"

"I asked him for it."

"Oh, sure! Nobody could get in to see the guy, or even reach him on the phone." His eyes narrowed. "You didn't promise Ray much. Maybe you're lying about the whole thing."

Pippa shrugged. "Okay, I'm lying."

Woody was clearly torn. "That fifty bucks said an *interview,* not a date. I'm not paying for any . . . overtime." His voice was unpleasantly suggestive.

Pippa controlled her anger, tipping her chair back against the wall. "You don't have to pay me anything—if you get the story first."

An ugly look crossed Woody's crafty face. "Fat chance! After you warned him off with a lot of stories about me."

Pippa shook her head in disbelief. "That's what you'd do, isn't it?"

"You can knock off the pious act," he snarled. "It's what *any* reporter worth the name would do. Don't start

44

congratulating yourself too soon though. I'm still top dog around here."

Pippa's lip curled in the semblance of a smile. "Well, you're half right."

"Pippa, do you have a phone number in your card file for Assemblyman Haynes?" Gloria called.

"She's busy," Woody snapped. "Look it up."

Pippa's chair clattered to the floor. "Who appointed you my secretary?"

"I was just doing the kid a favor," he replied urbanely. "You have to pull your own weight. The newsroom is a place for pros, not amateurs."

Pippa's blue eyes sparkled angrily. "I wasn't aware that providing a phone number was undue assistance."

"It's the principle of the thing. If Gloria is going to make it around here, she's going to have to start shaping up."

Pippa was aware that the whole newsroom was listening to their exchange. Her words were clear and carefully enunciated. "There is no question of Gloria making it. She is doing a very good job."

He shrugged, turning away. "If you say so."

"Woody!" Pippa's imperious tone stopped him in his tracks. "Just for my own edification, doesn't it ever bother you to shoot fish in a barrel?"

His lifted eyebrows were arrogant. "Meaning?"

"I was referring to your nonexistent sense of fair play."

Gloria joined them, her face apprehensive. "Pippa, I don't want—"

Pippa waved her to silence. "This really doesn't concern you, Gloria. I think Woody and I have just reached the point of no return."

Their eyes held as the newsroom grew quiet around them. "You'd better think twice about issuing challenges, Pippa," Woody said softly. "I've been here a lot longer than you have."

"But I'm in a better position," Pippa returned steadily. "I can go across the street to KYME tomorrow. Can you?"

Woody's eyes shifted uneasily. Through the years he had carved a niche for himself that was comfortable. He had grown lazy and complacent, skimming off the best stories to make himself look good. Pippa's advent changed all that. Her flair and professionalism forced Woody to recognize his vulnerability. In a showdown he wouldn't necessarily have the producer's backing. Woody was too streetwise not to be wary. He backed down, making light of the whole thing.

"Why would I want to do that? Or you either. Hey, we have an award-winning team here. We're like relatives."

Pippa wasn't fooled for a minute. "Then I'm sure you wouldn't want to see any other member of the family leave home either," she remarked caustically.

Woody struggled to remain friendly, succeeding only partially. Something ugly gleamed in his eyes. "You can't blame me if people come and go. Sometimes the young try their wings and fly away."

Pippa stared straight at him. "Just as long as they aren't *forced* out of the nest."

Ray came out of his office, and suddenly everyone got very busy. The strained atmosphere returned to normal.

Gloria watched Woody saunter away, her face troubled. "I didn't mean to get you mixed up in my problems. I never should have dumped on you last night."

"Don't worry about it." Pippa gave her a reassuring smile. "This thing has been brewing between Woody and me for months. You were only the unwitting catalyst."

"I don't want you to jeopardize your job over me."

"If it depended on getting along with Woody, it wouldn't be worth much. I'm a good reporter, Gloria, I can get a job anywhere. That's what I want *you* to remember, although it isn't going to come to that." Pippa gave her friend an impish grin. "If the two of us can't outmaneuver that aging roué, we'd better turn in our cards in the female sorority."

Gloria returned her smile tentatively. "I really appreciate your support. I just hope it isn't going to backfire on you."

For her part, Pippa was supremely confident. The showdown with Woody had to come sometime, and in what better cause than this? She didn't delude herself that it would bring a permanent improvement, but at least he had been put on warning.

It didn't bother Pippa that she had made a mortal enemy by causing him to lose face in front of the whole newsroom. What could he do to her? It was fortunate that she didn't know how much misery Woody would ultimately bring her.

CHAPTER THREE

Pippa had never looked forward so eagerly to the weekend. She scanned the weather reports with an anxious frown every day. It simply couldn't rain on Saturday!

Fortunately it didn't. Saturday was a bright, cloudless California day, with enough of a breeze to blow away the smog. Gazing out the window, Pippa's heart rose as high as the Hollywood hills that were sharply etched against the clear sky.

She spent a long time deciding what to wear, uncertain about how to change her image without scaring Jeremy off. It was aggravating to have to play an ingenue's role with this glamorous man. After selecting and rejecting numerous outfits, she finally settled on a white skirt topped by a printed silk blouse. The background of vivid blue was the color of her eyes. A pair of navy and white spectators and a dark blue cardigan completed her college-girl image.

The wind caught her carefully brushed pale brown hair as soon as she stepped out the door, ruffling it into a gold tipped cascade that rippled about her slim shoulders. With a sigh of resignation, Pippa swept it out of her eyes. The picture-perfect Calla probably never had a hair out of place, she thought irrelevantly. A wide grin suddenly curved Pippa's generous mouth as she remembered that

Calla was in San Francisco, and Jeremy was here—all hers today.

The motor entrance that separated the old hotel from the new addition was clogged with cars and taxis, since it was lunchtime. As Pippa idled in the queue she saw Jeremy come striding through the revolving door, his height making him instantly visible above the throng. Pippa noticed several women turn to stare—overtly or covertly, depending on their age. From their whispers and nudges she knew they were trying to figure out who he was—because it was obvious he was *somebody*.

He wore beige slacks and a cream-colored silk shirt under a tweedy jacket that emphasized the width of his powerful shoulders. An ascot was knotted casually around his bronze throat. Pippa felt a ripple of excitement as he crossed in front of the Mustang and opened the door on the driver's side.

"You're right on time," he greeted her approvingly.

"I'm always on time," she bragged.

"An admirable trait," he commented absently, fumbling with the lever that moved the seat back so he could straighten his long legs.

Pippa was slightly annoyed at the lack of warmth in his matter-of-fact greeting. She might have been a hired chauffeur for all the notice he took of her. "Your enthusiasm for this little outing is underwhelming," she remarked acidly. "I don't remember you as being quite this reserved."

He turned to look at her then, a frown pulling his dark brows together. "What's wrong, Pippa? If you've changed your mind about today, why don't you just come out and say so?"

Pippa's heart sank. After all the trouble it had taken to get him here, had she spoiled everything in a moment of pique? "I haven't!" she assured him hastily. "I was just afraid you had."

His grim expression relaxed. "I'm here," he pointed out.

"Well, couldn't you at least say it's nice to see me again
—even if you don't mean it?"

Jeremy was silent for a long moment, an unreadable
emotion in the green eyes that scanned her face. "The
trouble is, I do mean it," he said softly. His hand reached
out tentatively. "I like your hair this way."

His touch was so light she could barely feel it, but
Pippa's blood raced through her body. She wanted to
turn her head and feel those long fingers on her cheek. "It
isn't any special way," she murmured with difficulty.
"The wind—it must look a mess."

"It looks like you just got out of bed, all warm and
tousled." His low voice held a caressing note.

A taxi horn blared behind them, rudely pointing out
that the car ahead had moved out of the way. Jeremy
immediately put the Mustang in gear. As they drove out,
he turned a questioning eyebrow to Pippa. "Which way?"

She took a deep breath to steady herself. "Turn right,
then right again."

He followed directions, completely relaxed behind the
wheel. Pippa stole a glance at him out of the corner of her
eye. Why did he say things like that to her? He didn't
seem at all affected. Was it just to tease her? That must be
it. Pippa decided that she'd better get a grip on herself
and stop reacting like the college girl she was impersonat-
ing.

"We might as well stay on Wilshire Boulevard all the
way downtown," she told him. "It's the most scenic
route."

Jeremy drove the way he probably did everything else,
with practiced ease. Did he make love that competently
too? Pippa suppressed the errant thought, pointing out
landmarks along the way—the beautiful County Art Mu-
seum that was relatively new, and the stately Ambassa-
dor Hotel housing the famed Cocoanut Grove, that was
very old.

"Across the street was where the original Brown
Derby restaurant used to be, the one shaped like a hat.
People from out of town thought it was located in

Hollywood because it was always mentioned as a hangout for big stars in the golden age of movies. There was a terrible fuss when it was torn down recently."

Farther on they came to a beautiful lake ringed by palm trees and lawns that sloped down to the water's edge. Tall apartment houses and office buildings looked down on flocks of ducks swimming between little row boats manned by enthusiastic oarsmen. The broad boulevard curved around the lake, a calm oasis in the middle of the city.

"That looks like fun," Jeremy commented.

"It is," Pippa agreed. "One of my first boyfriends took me there. I'll never forget it."

"Why? Did he try to make love to you and tumble you both in the water?" he teased.

"Of course not! I was only thirteen. Is that all you ever think of?"

"You have a tendency to keep it in my mind," he said dryly.

"Then banish the thought completely," she told him curtly. "I don't intend to spend another night like I did last night. I could barely stand to look at myself in the mirror!"

Jeremy's green eyes darkened as they took in her flushed face. "Was the idea of my making love to you so repulsive?"

"That wasn't what I—" She stopped to compose herself.

The thought of what his lovemaking would be like caused a spreading warmth in the pit of her stomach. If the sample she'd been treated to was any criterion, Pippa didn't dare imagine further. In fact the whole idea was too mind-spinning to pursue.

"I'm beginning to think you're a very slick gent, Jeremy Hawke. All that talk about not wanting to get involved with me sounds like a monumental come-on. You've done nothing but make suggestive remarks since you got in this car!"

"You're right—about the remarks I mean." He shook

his head. "I'm afraid the exorcism isn't working. I find that I want you as much in daylight as I do at night." He turned to look at her, a frown creasing his wide brow. "Do you want me to turn around and take you back?"

"No, I . . . we . . . we might as well have lunch." She had this one afternoon to change his mind. Jeremy's decision not to see her again was evident in the deep lines that suddenly bracketed his firm mouth. If she didn't succeed in convincing him she was no threat, getting a story from him would be an impossibility.

Jeremy sighed. "I suppose you're right. I can't very well pounce on you in public."

"Oh, Jeremy, don't be silly! I know you've only been teasing me. It's my fault for taking you seriously." She ignored the ironic lift of his dark eyebrows. "Tell me how the investigation is going."

"It's too early," he answered evenly, accepting the change of subject. "We're still conducting preliminary interviews."

"Lots of luck with Willie Maybeck; he's a wily little brute." The corners of Pippa's mouth turned down as she remembered the assemblyman's inability to answer even a simple question directly.

Jeremy's eyes narrowed. "What do you know about Maybeck?"

Too late Pippa realized her mistake. "Nothing really. I . . . his name came up in poly sci class. We went over his published interviews, and he didn't seem too, uh, direct. Have you spoken to him?"

"I imagine I'll be in contact with half of Los Angeles before this is over," Jeremy replied smoothly, giving nothing away.

"Really, Jeremy, you don't have to be so cagey!" Pippa couldn't control her irritation. "The whole town knows that little Willie's been on the take for years! Why else would he be the swing vote that awarded the contract to a little Mickey Mouse outfit like Carl Dabney's, when there are more qualified contractors?"

"That political science class of yours seems remarkably well informed," Jeremy said softly.

Pippa caught the corner of her lip in small, white teeth. "I guess I get rather carried away sometimes." She looked at him out of the corner of her eye. "I can't help feeling involved though. If I were a little older and had children, they could very easily have gone to that school."

Jeremy's warm hand covered her nervous fingers. "I know what you mean. I feel the same way, even though I don't live here." His face hardened. "That's why we're going to get to the bottom of this."

"Wouldn't you like to talk about it?" she suggested.

"Isn't that Olvera Street up ahead?" The fact that he was correct made Pippa uncertain about whether Jeremy would have pursued the subject or not. "Where do we park?" he asked.

In the attendant flurry of finding a parking lot and an empty space, all talk of the investigation was inevitably shelved. And when they walked around the corner to "the oldest street in Los Angeles," Jeremy's attention couldn't be diverted.

The brick-paved lane was indeed charming, living up to its reputation as a bit of old Mexico. Shops and restaurants lined each side, with a row of open-air booths down the center. The wares displayed were colorful beyond belief—gaily decorated pottery, brightly painted baskets, some in the shape of animals, striped mariachis, feathered birds, and much, much more.

Jeremy picked up a crepe paper animal of improbable origin, fashioned in loops of orange, red, and black. "What on earth would you do with this?"

"It's a piñata," Pippa told him. "See the hollow in the tummy? At Christmas time it's a Mexican tradition to fill a piñata with small presents and hang it from the ceiling. The little children whack away at it until the presents rain down."

Jeremy was charmed, selecting the biggest one he could find. Then he bought her a woven hat with bright straw flowers on the brim. When he lingered over some papier mâché figures of acrobats perched on each other's shoulders, Pippa laughingly dragged him away.

"Let's have lunch before you spend all your money," she cried.

They found an open air café, selecting a table on the sidewalk so they could watch the passing parade. Pippa helped him with the menu, bypassing the ordinary tacos and tamales in favor of empanadillas, delightful little pillow-shaped pastries filled with cheese. With them she ordered carne asada, a grilled steak covered with spicy sauce. Jeremy ate with a hearty appetite, cooling down his mouth with frequent gulps of Mexican beer.

"Why haven't I heard about this before?" he asked between bites.

"It isn't fancy enough for you," Pippa replied, buttering a hot tortilla. "Your stomach is probably in shock. It was expecting French haute cuisine."

"That shows how much you know. My stomach accommodates everything except raw fish."

"Then I'm glad I didn't order ceviche." She grinned. "That's raw fillets marinated in lime juice. The fish is cured until it's pure white, then served with tomatoes and green peppers and stuff. It's really a delicious dish."

"How delicious would it be without the tomatoes, green peppers, and 'stuff'?" he asked dryly. "Don't bother to answer. I've avoided raw fish in Japanese restaurants at home; if it's all the same to you, I'll go on doing it."

"When you say home, I gather you mean San Francisco?"

Jeremy nodded. "Or, more precisely, Woodside. It's about twenty miles from the city—very rural and woodsy, as the name implies."

Pippa looked him over. Even in casual clothes Jeremy Hawke was the picture of sophistication and elegance. "I can't quite see you as a country squire."

"Appearances are deceiving." His voice dropped a note. "As you of all people should know."

She avoided his mocking eyes. "It's interesting that you still regard California as home."

"It always will be," he said simply.

"Don't you like Washington?"

Jeremy shrugged. "It has its compensations, but I never intended to live there permanently. When my job is finished, I'll be back."

"Did you ever consider running for office?" He'd certainly get all the female vote! Pippa had noticed how women passing their sidewalk table had stolen surreptitious glances at the tall, broad-shouldered man with the unusual green eyes and the sensuous mouth. His blatant masculinity ensnared even strangers.

"Good Lord, no!" He answered her question with an emphatic negative. "I can't think of anything I'd hate more."

"You're working for the government *now,*" she pointed out.

"A different thing entirely. I'm conducting a private investigation, or at least trying to," he noted grimly. "The result won't be influenced by a need to win votes, or a desire for publicity."

"You really don't like being in the public eye, do you?" she asked slowly.

"No, I don't." His answer was clipped. "That's for entertainers—or people who need it for their ego."

"Still, by taking on this job, you have no right to avoid it completely," Pippa replied stubbornly. "How about the public's right to know?"

Jeremy's lip curled contemptuously. "A classic media cop-out; you parrot it very well. But how about the rights of the people under investigation? Don't the innocent deserve a chance to be cleared before being tainted forevermore by the mere *suspicion* of wrongdoing?"

"Of course, but—"

"And how about the right of the public to a fair shake? Is it reasonable for an investigation to be jeopardized just to fill up a lot of pulp paper, or to give a blithering newscaster something to read off a monitor?"

"You act as though all reporters are the enemy," Pippa said hotly. "There are ethics in the news industry like anywhere else."

Jeremy's eyes were chips of green glass. "If there are, I've never run across them."

"That's patently unfair! How can you indict a whole profession?"

"Because I have the battle scars to prove my contention." His mouth curved derisively before straightening to a thin line. "I've told you the stratagems the media have employed to harass me."

"Only because you're uncooperative," she protested. "I can't believe *everything* is top secret. If you'd part with just a little information, they wouldn't hound you so much."

"You don't honestly believe that?"

"Yes, I do. You can't blame them for trying to do their job. It's just as honorable in its way as yours is."

Jeremy raised his eyes to the sky. "Why am I arguing with a starry-eyed innocent?" He fixed her with a stern gaze. "Do you have any idea what those noble people you're defending would give to be sitting where you are right now? To be able to catch me in an unguarded moment when I might reveal some nugget of classified information?"

Pippa looked down at the bread crumb she was rolling around and around in her slim fingers. "No decent newsperson would take advantage of you like that."

"The two words aren't synonymous," he said dryly. "No, my dear, I'm afraid reporters and I are natural enemies."

Her downcast eyelashes fluttered. "Maybe if you actually got to know one, you'd change your mind."

Jeremy chuckled. "That's right, you're a journalism major, aren't you? I'd almost forgotten. No wonder your defense was so impassioned. It hasn't changed my mind though."

"But look how well we've gotten along—for the most part," she faltered at his wholly male expression.

"It isn't the same thing. You came to me for an auto-graph, not a story." His eyes narrowed suddenly on her flushed face. "That *is* why you came, isn't it, Pippa? Or was it actually for an interview for your campus newspa-per?"

At least he still believed she was a student. Pippa felt a shiver go up her spine, sensing what thin ice she was treading. Somehow she managed to meet his searching gaze. "I told you I don't have a place on the paper." She forced a smile. "Although, if you'd give me an interview, I'm sure I could get one."

Jeremy relaxed. "You're incorrigible." He laughed. "Thank God you're *not* a reporter. I'd probably tell you anything you wanted to know."

Pippa bit her lip, troubled blue eyes fixed on him ear-nestly. "I wouldn't use it if it were off the record, Jer-emy."

He covered her hand with his large warm one, squeez-ing her fingers gently. "Try and keep that integrity, honey. You're too nice a person to ever descend to their level."

Pippa had never felt quite so despicable in her life. If Jeremy knew the truth, his contempt would be too terri-ble to contemplate. What she had told him was true, that she would never betray a confidence. He wouldn't believe it, though, not after the way she had lied and schemed to meet him. The trouble was that the story was gradually fading in importance—and that was a first in her journal-istic career. It was Jeremy's good opinion that had be-come the primary consideration.

In just a short time he had managed to thoroughly intrigue her. Not that she was falling in love with him, or anything foolish like that. It was just that he was a fasci-nating man she would like to know better. There weren't very many men with his combination of good looks, intel-ligence, and humor. Why did she have to ruin everything because of that stupid bet with Woody? It was too late to do anything about it now though. She would have to let him walk out of her life without ever getting to know him. Pippa sighed heavily.

"Hey, don't look so unhappy, little one." Jeremy's long forefinger lifted her chin. "I'm sorry I denigrated your chosen profession."

"It's all right." Pippa mustered a smile. "Maybe I'll switch to electronics so we can agree on something."

His long fingers gently stroked her cheek. "I may be a male chauvinist as you secretly believe, but it doesn't go that far. I don't want you to pay me lip service—at least not that way." He grinned briefly before becoming serious again. "You're bright, and sweet, and fun to be with. Don't change for anyone."

Pippa felt a constriction in her throat. "I just wish . . ."

When she didn't finish, Jeremy said, "What do you wish, honey?"

"Oh, nothing. It isn't important. Do you want to go through the rest of the shops?"

As they wandered up and down the short street, Pippa's tension gradually lessened. Only once did it return, when she caught her high heel in the uneven paving. Jeremy reached out immediately, saving her from a fall. His strong arm around her waist was steadying, holding her against his hard, lean body for a breathless instant.

Pippa's hands went to his broad shoulders, feeling their muscular width through the soft fabric of his sport coat. For an enchanted moment in time she remained in his arms, lifting her face to his like a flower thirsty for the sun. Jeremy caught his breath, lowering his head.

Suddenly they were jolted by a little boy on a skateboard. "Sorry," the child trilled, racing away, completely unaware of what he had destroyed.

Jeremy released her immediately. "Are you all right?" His deep voice was a little ragged.

"Yes, I . . . this brick is murder on high heels." Pippa avoided looking at him.

CHAPTER FIVE

Pippa's misery was intensified the next day when she went into the newsroom. Woody was just waiting to pounce.

"Well, how was your date with the Hawke?" he asked mockingly.

Her heart almost stopped beating until she realized he was talking about Saturday. "Very satisfactory," she answered tersely, shuffling some papers around to indicate she was busy.

He didn't take the hint. "Did you get anything that can go out over the air?"

"Since when have you been appointed to Ray's job?" she asked coolly.

"Since I have fifty bucks riding on that story."

"Oh, for heaven's sake!" Pippa exclaimed impatiently. "If I'd known it was going to keep you up nights, I wouldn't have let you risk the thing you're fondest of."

"It isn't the money, it's the chance to cut you off at the knees. You've been getting too big for those tight jeans lately."

Pippa's face wore a look of supreme confidence. "I wouldn't build a coop for that chicken yet."

Her assurance shook him. "I wonder if you knew the guy before. It doesn't seem possible that you—" Woody's eyes narrowed. "Did you sucker me into this thing?"

It was a golden opportunity, which Pippa seized swiftly. "Okay, Woody, I'll let you off the hook, since that's what you're obviously fishing for. We'll call off the bet."

His face held suspicion. "When did you start taking generosity pills?"

She shrugged. "It's worth foregoing the fifty dollars to get you off my back." If Pippa had left it there, that might have been the end of it. But she got anxious. "Besides, I think the man is entitled to his privacy," she added carelessly.

Woody's pouched eyes gleamed like a pit bull's going for the jugular. "Freely translated, that means you're not getting anywhere. No deal, Pippa, the bet's still on. Unless you'd like to pay me right now and get it over with."

It was a temptation. Maybe then she could go about the business of forgetting a tall, lean man named Jeremy Hawke. Woody would crow about it for weeks, but she could live with that more easily than with her memories. His next words put her right back in the trap.

"I think I'll send Hawke a thank-you note telling him what he did for me," Woody declared.

Pippa's blood chilled at the thought of Jeremy finding out about her in that way. "Who are you going to get to write it for you?" she asked scornfully. "You've never thanked anyone for anything in your life."

"Temper, temper," he chided mockingly. "You wouldn't want me to tell your boyfriend that you're a bad loser on top of being a lousy reporter."

Pippa's eyes locked with his. "I'd tell you that someday you'll go too far, Woody, except that *no* place would be far enough. Now, go slither under something and let me get to work."

Alone at her desk, Pippa reached a new low. There was no way she could get that interview—although the only reason it mattered now was to keep Woody from betraying her. Even if she could put herself through that torture, Jeremy would never see her again. Still, she had to try. The chances were laughably remote, but it was the only course open.

Pippa realized she didn't have the luxury of putting it off either. Although the wounds from last night were still fresh and bleeding, once Jeremy moved out of the hotel he would be lost to her.

She waited till six o'clock, the most logical time to catch him. He should be back from work by then. Pippa's hands were icy as she dialed the number. Her heart was thundering so loudly that she wondered if she'd be able to hear his voice. It wasn't Jeremy who answered the phone, however.

"Mr. Hawke is in a meeting right now," a man informed her. "Can I take a message?"

Pippa experienced a mixture of relief and letdown. "Would you please tell him that Pippa Alcott called."

"Certainly, Miss Alcott. Is that with one *L* or two?"

Suddenly she heard Jeremy's deep voice in the background. After a few terse questions to the man, he said, "I'll take it on the extension in the bedroom." A moment later he was on the line. "What can I do for you, Pippa?"

His crisp, no-nonsense voice wasn't reassuring. She might have been a bill collector for all the warmth that was present. But he had taken her call, she reminded herself. Didn't that prove something?

"Pippa?" he asked sharply. "Are you there?"

"Yes, I—I'm here," she answered lamely. "I hope I'm not disturbing you."

"Since when did that bother you?" he asked dryly.

"You don't have to be nasty about it!" she replied hotly.

"Would you care to tell me why you're calling?"

She could almost see the grim set of his jaw. If Pippa had secretly harbored any hope of a tender reunion, it died a sudden death. Her anger rose swiftly. What did he have to feel so injured about? Knowing there wasn't any point in it, she played the last card in her hand.

"I have something that belongs to you," she informed him stiffly.

"What would that be?"

"Your shirt."

"What are you talking about?" he asked blankly. "Oh . . ."

Pippa gripped the phone tightly as she imagined the memories that were coming back to him. "I've had it laundered and I want to bring it back to you."

"I don't need it. Keep it for a souvenir," he told her mockingly.

"That's only for things you want to remember," she remarked pointedly. "I have to come over anyway. You still have my blouse, and I do want it back. I presume the valet returned it?"

"Yes, it's hanging in my closet. It still smells of your perfume," he said softly.

"I'm sorry if that's unpleasant for you. I'll come over and get it right away, if that's all right."

"Unfortunately, it isn't. We were just about to go out to dinner."

"I could drop by tomorrow night," she suggested, hating the thought of what the delay would do to her nerves.

"Well, the thing is, I'm moving to Malibu in the morning."

Pippa recognized the brush-off. "All right, Jeremy," she sighed. "Forget the whole thing. I'll see you around."

"Wait!" he called tautly. "If you want to drive that far, you can pick up your blouse there." His offhand tone contrasted with his urgency of a moment ago.

"I suppose I could do that," she remarked with equal indifference. "It isn't that far, really. When would be convenient for you?"

"Tomorrow night about this time?"

"Fine." Her tone was carefully businesslike. "See you then."

"Pippa . . ." She paused in the act of hanging up. "I do owe you a meal," Jeremy said. "Would you like to come for dinner?"

"No!" Her refusal was instant and vehement.

There would be no candlelight seduction, she promised

herself. This was going to be strictly business—an attempt to get Jeremy out of her life while preserving her integrity.

His low chuckle revealed his amusement. "That sounded pretty definite."

"It was. I don't want to spend an evening alone with you any more than you do with me."

"It isn't a question of what I want," he answered somberly.

"I'll make it easy for you. I'll be at your place at six, and out by six fifteen."

"How about if there were other people there?" he asked abruptly. "This house is right on the beach. We could all go for a moonlight swim after dinner."

The whole thing was so unexpected that Pippa was momentarily at a loss. "Who would be there?"

"My aides, and maybe some of their girlfriends."

That would mean local girls who might recognize her name, but Pippa decided to chance it. The gain far outweighed the risk. In the relaxed atmosphere of a group, Jeremy might be persuaded to give her an interview about completely nonessential things. She no longer even wanted anything more—just to write *finis* to a painful mistake.

"I guess that would be all right," she said grudgingly.

"Good. Bring your bathing suit. I'll see you tomorrow night." He gave her the address and was all business once more.

The news was half over before Pippa even remembered the show was going on. Fortunately all the wire services were quiet. She would have been hard put to handle a minor story, let alone a disaster. Her mind was on other things.

She would have to ask Gloria to fill in for her tomorrow night. It was better than a half-hour drive to Malibu from her apartment, and the newscast wasn't over until seven. Ray would give her the time off if he knew the reason, but she was reluctant to bring any more people in on this.

The sun was setting the next evening as Pippa drove up to the low redwood-and-glass house overlooking the beach. Daylight was following the fire-red ball that almost seemed to hiss as it slipped into the dark blue water.

She parked the Mustang next to the other cars in the driveway, reaching for the tote bag that held her bikini and beach sandals. After tucking her striped T-shirt into the waistband of her white slacks, Pippa headed for the front door.

A rather taciturn woman in a maid's uniform answered her ring. She was probably an excellent servant, but her personality left a lot to be desired, Pippa decided. After directing her toward the other guests, the housekeeper disappeared into the kitchen.

The living room was at the back of the house, facing the beach. Through the wide glass windows she could see that the party was gathered for cocktails on the deck outside. There were two men and a woman besides Jeremy. But for Pippa, he was the only one there.

Her breathing was uneven as she stared at the man she had fallen so foolishly in love with. He had on pale gray slacks and a checked shirt open to his waistband, exposing dark hair that inched in a V down his tan chest. With his flashing white smile he looked like a pirate—bold, and incredibly handsome. Pippa drew a deep breath, arming herself for whatever was to come.

Jeremy's casual greeting gave no indication that there had ever been anything between them. He introduced her to the others, remarking, "You shouldn't have any trouble remembering Stretch's name."

It was obvious where Jeremy's chief assistant got his nickname. He was long and lanky, even taller than Jeremy, but without his splendid physique. Stretch was in his late twenties, Pippa judged, with a pleasant, outgoing personality and a nice sense of humor.

"The chief didn't tell us you were beautiful," he complained.

That figured. "What *did* he tell you?" Pippa asked.

Rick Murphy, the other aide who was about the same age, answered for him, giving her a teasing smile. "He said we should be on our toes because he'd invited a very bright college girl who was going to hit us up for an interview for her college paper."

"Maybe you could convince him to let me have it," Pippa said without looking at Jeremy.

Rita Whitehall, Rick's date, spoiled the opportunity. "What school do you go to, Pippa?"

Pippa told her, sighing inwardly. Well, the evening was young.

"I spent a year at U.C.L.A. before I transferred to art school," Rita told her. "Is that weird psychology professor still there? You know who I mean—the one who was so popular they had to hold his classes in a lecture hall."

Pippa smiled. "Are you talking about the one who told all the kids to go out and do it? He got into a little trouble after he went out and did it with one of his students."

That sparked a flood of reminiscences as the others harked back to their college days. All except Jeremy. Pippa was acutely conscious of the fact that he didn't join in the conversation. Jeremy lounged in a deck chair, regarding them with the indulgent smile of a grown-up chaperoning a group of teenagers. Was that why he had invited her? To point up the difference in their ages and interests? And was it only a coincidence that Stretch had no date tonight—or was he supposed to be Pippa's date?

Dinner was a barbecue that Jeremy presided over, cooking thick steaks to charred perfection on an outdoor grill. Mrs. Dunphy, the housekeeper, unobtrusively set the round redwood table and supplied the rest of the meal. Her personality was so colorless that she seemed to fade into the background. No one took any notice of her.

Over dinner Rick remarked casually, "You don't look like a college girl, Pippa."

While applauding his perception, she recognized the danger. "What do I look like?" she asked in an offhand way.

"A very foxy lady," Stretch answered for him.

Jeremy's light eyes were enigmatic. "I've never known exactly what that meant."

Stretch grinned at Pippa, as though sharing a joke. "It's called the generation gap."

He couldn't know he was hammering nails into her coffin. "Jeremy isn't that much older," she said carefully.

Jeremy's smile was sardonic. "You don't have to champion my cause, Pippa. I've reconciled myself to my advanced state of senility."

"Hardly that, boss. I've seen you in action." Stretch's eyes were admiring. "You're quite an operator."

"When I'm playing in my own league," Jeremy answered dryly. "Youngsters confuse me."

Pippa had taken enough of his hidden barbs. "Only because you're afraid to take a chance!" she cried. "Your dream girl has to be a certain height, a certain weight—a certain age!" When a small silence greeted her heated words, Pippa realized she was revealing too much. She gave a little laugh. "But thank goodness for confirmed bachelors like you. Where else would we find that extra man to take out our visiting cousin from Peoria?"

"That's one of the liabilities of being single," Rick grinned. "Those visiting female cousins."

"She isn't exactly pretty, but she has a great personality," Stretch mimicked in a high falsetto.

In the ensuing laughter the tension was dissolved, but Pippa was aware of Jeremy's unintelligible gaze.

"Why is it all men expect a cross between Helen of Troy and Marilyn Monroe on a blind date?" Rita complained.

"Because hope springs eternal," Stretch told her. His admiring eyes went to Pippa. "Although sometimes it's justified. Tell me about your dreams and ambitions, Pippa."

So it was true that she was supposed to be Stretch's date. A crushing sense of defeat enveloped Pippa. She pinned a determined smile on her face. "My ambition is to get an interview out of Jeremy."

"Why don't you give the kid a break?" Rick chuckled indulgently.

"Sure, what would it hurt?" Stretch urged.

"Perhaps the whole investigation," Jeremy answered grimly.

"I'm not asking for classified information." Pippa raised her chin, looking squarely at him. "What you had for breakfast will do."

His eyes held hers. "Pecan waffles with maple syrup," he replied softly. "I'll never forget it."

"Stop snowing the poor girl," Stretch protested. "We all had breakfast together and it was less than memorable —a stale Danish and lukewarm coffee."

"You have no romance in your soul," Jeremy remarked mockingly. "I was telling her what she wanted to hear."

The pain that shot through her at his derisive statement was devastating. That day together had meant nothing to him. "You don't have to sugar-coat anything for me," she said bitterly. "I'm perfectly capable of facing reality."

"Are you, Pippa? I don't think so." Deep lines carved themselves alongside his mouth. "I believe you live for the moment, without counting the cost—or what will happen when the bells stop ringing."

"At least I'm not afraid to live. That brings only regrets. Today will never come again."

"You're like the man who said he had enough money to live on the rest of his life—if he died tomorrow."

They were oblivious to the others, locked in their private battle.

"Hey, you two, lighten up," Stretch said. "You're not going to settle the battle of youth versus experience tonight. What say we go swimming?"

Pippa saw her opportunity slipping away. Now more than ever she had to sever all ties to Jeremy. "He hasn't said he'll give me an interview. *Please,* Jeremy. I promise never to bother you again!"

93

His smile was twisted. "If I thought that could be accomplished, I'd be tempted."

Stretch took Pippa's hands, pulling her to her feet. "You're gaining on him. Let's go swimming. After he's in a weakened condition you can close in for the kill."

Pippa followed Rita into one of the bedrooms, feeling utterly drained.

"I'm afraid you have your work cut out for you with Jeremy," Rita commented, stripping off her T-shirt. "It won't be easy to change his mind."

"I have to," Pippa answered desperately.

The other woman looked at her curiously. "Does it mean that much to you?"

"More than you know!"

There was a knock at the door. Rita put on her beach robe to answer it, finding Rick with a tray holding two snifters of brandy.

"Compliments of the management," he grinned.

"Well, I must say Jeremy is the perfect host," Rita commented, offering a glass to Pippa.

"I really don't think I should." Pippa was still feeling the effects of one cocktail and the wine with dinner, since she had been too tense to eat.

"It'll relax you," Rita assured her. "That go-around with Jeremy has you tied up in knots."

That was certainly true! Pippa sipped the brandy as she got into her bikini, finding that it did indeed relax her. By the time they joined the men, her spirits had lifted.

The bonfire they had lit on the beach was to provide warmth after they came out of the water. In the light of the dancing flames, Jeremy's bronze body held Pippa's eyes. He looked like a Greek god, his tapering torso and long, lean legs perfectly sculpted. The brief white trunks that were his only covering merely enhanced his masculinity.

"Okay, troops, hear this. You're all to stay within hailing distance of shore," Jeremy ordered.

"What are you going to do if we don't, spank us?" Pippa chortled, spurred on by the brandy.

His expression changed as he looked at her curved body, provocatively revealed by the two little scraps of cloth. "Don't tempt me, lady."

Pippa tilted her head. "You'll have to catch me first."

She raced toward the water. After a brief moment Jeremy followed, catching her easily. His arms closed around her waist as he tripped her, throwing them both to the sand.

"I give up," she giggled.

"Oh, no, it's not that easy. You have to pay for your sins."

"I said I was sorry," she pleaded in mock alarm. "What more do you want?"

The laughter in his eyes died as he looked down at her, his hard body half covering hers. The flames were reflected in his eyes, turning them to glowing coals. "You know the answer to that."

Pippa's breathing quickened. Her hands moved slowly over his shoulders, feeling the shifting muscles as he drew her closer.

"Hey, stop roughing up my date." Stretch's laughing protest destroyed the moment.

Jeremy released her immediately, getting to his feet in one lithe movement. "You're right, I should know better," he muttered. Turning away abruptly, he waded into the ocean, striking out to sea with powerful strokes.

"Evidently that rule about staying close to shore doesn't apply to our host," Rita commented.

"Jeremy is a law unto himself," Rick told her. He frowned slightly, staring out at the strong swimmer. "Although it isn't like him to take reckless chances."

"You're so right," Pippa remarked bitterly.

Stretch put his arm around her shoulders. "Don't worry, little Pippa, we'll get you that interview yet."

When they were all sitting around the fire later, the conversation turned to surfing.

"It's better farther up the coast," Pippa informed Stretch after he had expressed an interest. "The waves are higher at Zuma Beach."

"How about coming with me this weekend?" he asked.

"I can't, I have to work," she answered without thinking. Suddenly conscious of their surprised expressions, Pippa tried to retrieve her error. "I'm going to study. Finals are coming up and I've been goofing off lately."

"A very apt way of putting it," Jeremy murmured from the shadows where he was watching her.

Pippa was glad she couldn't see the mocking expression on his face.

"The fire's starting to die down," Stretch said. "Should I scrounge around for some more driftwood?"

Jeremy stood up, the languishing flames gilding his long limbs. "You young people can carry on if you like. I'm going to organize my schedule for tomorrow and then hit the sack."

"I think it's time we all got going," Rick decided. "We still have a drive ahead of us."

"I'll ride back with Pippa so she doesn't have that long trip alone." Stretch gave her a mischievous grin. "I might even convince her to show me where the local college kids go to neck."

"Boy, are *you* behind the times," Rick hooted. "Kids don't make out in parked cars anymore."

"Really?" Stretch raised his eyebrows in mock surprise. "There goes my whole game plan."

Pippa laughed. "I'm sure you'll think of another."

Jeremy didn't join in the playful banter. His expression was enigmatic as he watched them gather together towels and beach robes.

"I'll get my briefcase out of Rick's car before I forget," Stretch remarked.

"That won't be necessary," Jeremy said abruptly. "I've decided to give Pippa her interview, so you'd better go back with him." His austere face discouraged any comment.

Pippa's emotions at this announcement were decidedly mixed. There was relief that it would all be over soon, yet apprehension at being alone with Jeremy.

As soon as they reached the house she sat down at a

card table in the living room without going to change. If she hurried Jeremy along, perhaps they could complete the interview while the others were getting dressed. Then she'd ask Stretch to wait. It would only take a minute to throw on her slacks over the bikini.

Her plan was thwarted by Mrs. Dunphy, who claimed Jeremy's attention in the kitchen for a seemingly endless length of time.

"Sorry," he said when he returned. "This is her first day and she had a lot of questions before she left."

"Doesn't she live in?" Pippa asked.

"There's no need. I never eat breakfast at home."

Before she could get him back on the subject, the others started drifting in.

The house seemed achingly quiet after they had all left.

Pippa tried to ignore it. "Is this going to be a progress report, or some personal anecdotes?" she asked in her most professional manner.

Jeremy's face was grim. "You know how I hate that sort of thing."

"Then you're going to tell me what you've uncovered?" She felt a thrill of anticipation in spite of herself.

He raised a sardonic eyebrow. "Do you really expect me to?"

It was like having a prize snatched away at the last second. "I'm not a fiction writer!" she cried in exasperation. "If you won't tell me how the investigation is proceeding, and you aren't willing to talk about yourself, why did you say you'd give me an interview?"

"I didn't want you to leave with Stretch," he replied somberly.

"You mean you let me get my hopes up for no good reason?" Pippa was furious.

"I've just given you the reason."

"I don't believe you! How could you be so rotten?"

His smile was self-mocking. "You seem to bring out the worst in me."

She pushed her chair back, anger in every rigid line of

her slight body. "I'm glad you think it's amusing. Too bad I don't share your warped sense of humor."

A muscle jerked at the point of Jeremy's square jaw. "You're wrong, my dear. I don't find one damn thing funny about this situation."

"Well, if anything occurs to you, don't bother to tell me."

As she turned away, his arm curled around her waist, seeming to scorch her bare skin. "I don't want you to go, Pippa."

"You don't know *what* you want," she flared.

His voice was husky as he drew her closer. "That was never the problem."

Pippa held him off, trying not to notice how smooth and warm his skin felt. "Let me go, Jeremy. I'm leaving."

"I can't let you." He imprisoned her between his knees, bending his head to kiss the satin skin of her stomach before his tongue dipped into her navel.

She tried without success to twist out of his tantalizing embrace. "You don't have any choice," she gasped.

"I realize that now." His fingertips trailed erotic patterns over the bare skin between her bra and bikini bottoms. "I was lost the minute you walked into my hotel room."

"God, how I wish I never had!" she groaned.

"Me too," he murmured, holding her against his chest while he untied the string that fastened her bra. "But we both know it's too late for regrets."

The scrap of cloth fell away, leaving her small, high breasts exposed to his glittering eyes. Jeremy touched her almost reverently, his exploring fingertips sending a thrill through her entire body. When he took one nipple between his lips, tasting it with the tip of his tongue, Pippa's fingernails dug unconsciously into his shoulders.

"Nothing's changed," she warned him despairingly. "I'm the same person you walked out on before."

"Not tonight." He didn't give her the reassurance she was yearning for. "Tonight I'm going to make love to you a hundred different ways."

"And tomorrow?" She tried to capture the fingers that reached for the bottom of her bikini. "How will you deal with your regrets?"

"There is no tomorrow," he growled, tossing aside her bikini bottom and sweeping her nude body into his arms.

All of the arguments Pippa knew to be valid fled before the inexpressible feeling. She curled up against him, clasping her arms around his neck.

Jeremy's mouth claimed hers in a kiss so drugging that she scarcely realized he was carrying her into the bedroom. He set her gently on the bed, pausing only a second to remove his trunks before joining her. His hands trailed lingeringly down her body, lighting a slow fire that his mouth fanned into a roaring inferno.

Pippa arched against him, running her fingers through his crisp hair while she murmured his name. His arms tightened and he drew her hips against his so she could feel the strength of his passion. She shuddered with the force of her desire, moving restlessly against him with a consuming need.

Her response intensified Jeremy's own need. His tongue explored her mouth with a driving masculinity that promised ultimate ecstasy, while his caresses became more fervent. When his knee parted her legs, Pippa welcomed him with a sigh of fulfillment, accepting him into the very core of her being.

Jeremy was an ardent lover, carrying her with him to heights so dizzying that she quivered with pure rapture. When they reached the summit together, waves of pleasure washed over her, filling the aching void that had cried out for him. She clung tightly to him as they drifted back to earth, totally satisfied.

Jeremy held her in his arms, burying his face in her neck. After a long time he raised his head to look at her, tenderly smoothing the silky hair from her face. "My beautiful Pippa. We've wasted so much time."

She traced the strong line of his jaw before biting his earlobe playfully. "That's what I was trying to tell you."

"Never mind." He gave her a slow smile, curving his hand possessively around her breast. "I plan to make up for it."

CHAPTER SIX

Pippa awoke the next morning, still cradled in Jeremy's
arms. It had been a night of love such as she couldn't
even have imagined. Their hunger for each other had
been so great that they had both reached out repeatedly,
erasing all the frustrations that had marred their previous
relationship.

Pippa's soft mouth curved in a smile as she relived the
rapturous moments. She examined Jeremy's beloved face,
relaxed now in sleep. Who could believe this autocratic
man could be so tender and thoughtful? She longed to
kiss those firm lips whose touch had driven her into a
frenzy, but she stopped herself for fear of waking him. It
was enough for now just to be in the arms of the man she
loved.

Pippa's smile faltered as she realized that through the
whole ecstatic night Jeremy had never said he loved her.
He had told her she was beautiful, ravishing, that she
drove him out of his mind with wanting her, but he had
never said the three important words. Was she putting
undue emphasis on it? Or was it intentional on Jeremy's
part? He had his own kind of integrity. Was he trying to
tell her something?

As she stirred uneasily, Jeremy opened his eyes. He
pulled her back against his sleep-warmed body, murmur-

ing huskily, "Come here to me. I need to touch you so I'm sure you're real."

"You should know that by now," she teased, cuddling up against him.

"Let me hold you. I was afraid I dreamed the whole thing." His hands wandered over all her secret places.

An answering warmth drove away Pippa's apprehensions. "Do you usually have such erotic dreams?" She smiled impishly.

He blew softly in her ear. "Whenever I think of you." His legs twined around hers, making her aware of his desire.

"It's getting late; we both have to drive into the city." Pippa's half-hearted protest died as Jeremy slid her body under his.

They showered together afterward, "to save time" as Jeremy put it. Pippa wasn't fooled, nor would she have had it any other way. It was a glorious experience, running her soapy hands over his superb male frame.

Although it really was getting late by then, they took time to have coffee out on the deck. It was a sparkling morning, with a light breeze that stirred up little lace-trimmed wavelets on the surface of the blue water.

Pippa had never been this happy in her life. She looked possessively at Jeremy, pretending just for now that they were married and this was their home. It was a childish game, but she couldn't help it.

He tipped her chin up, smiling down at her tenderly. "Can I hope I'm responsible for that glow in your eyes?"

"I can't remember being with anyone else last night," she teased.

"I don't want you to be with anyone else *any* night." As Pippa's heart started to sing, Jeremy said, "Will you stay with me so we can have as much time together as possible while I'm here?"

Her heart did a rapid nosedive. Was that all she meant to him, a girl for the duration? Her long eyelashes lowered to hide the deep hurt.

"Pippa? Is something wrong, honey?" His deep voice was filled with concern.

"I was just thinking over your proposition," she answered brightly.

He frowned. "It wasn't a proposition."

She was on the point of asking what he would call it when she stopped. Pippa didn't want to quarrel with him, not now of all times. Besides, it wasn't Jeremy's fault if she had adolescent dreams of love and marriage. He had certainly never encouraged her in that direction. If this was all she was destined to have, well, so be it. Pippa knew she would rather have a short time with Jeremy than a lifetime with any other man.

That brought up another point. Under the circumstances, there was no reason to tell him the truth about herself. He might as well go on thinking of her as the happy-go-lucky college girl who didn't have a care in the world. She couldn't move in here though. Nor could she afford to be seen in her usual haunts with him. This would have to be a secret idyl, unmarred by contact with the outside world.

"I can't live with you, Jeremy," she said reluctantly. "You're too well-known. The media would be on it like a shot, and it wouldn't be good for either of us." While that excuse was true, it took care of her problems.

"I'm not going to give you up," he warned.

"I don't want you to," she said hastily. "We'll just have to be a little discreet."

The disgust on his face gave Jeremy's opinion of that idea. "I want you with me. I want to go to sleep with you in my arms, and wake up the same way."

He would never know how much she agreed! "We'll work it out," she temporized. "You'd better get going now, or Stretch and Rick will send out a posse."

"I suppose you're right," he sighed. "I'll see you tonight." It wasn't a suggestion, it was a command. "We'll go out to dinner. At some quiet place," he added before she could object.

Another problem occurred to Pippa. She didn't get off

work until the news was over at seven. The longer drive from Hollywood would make it at least eight. That was rather late to be at a class. Well, there was no help for it.

"The trouble is, I'm taking an accounting course," she told him. "It was so crowded that they had to add an additional class from six to seven. I couldn't get here until eight." Pippa wondered wildly how she was going to explain away her unavailability on weekends. She decided to cross that bridge when she came to it.

"Why don't I pick you up at school? We can eat someplace in the city."

"No, don't do that! I—I'll get here as soon as I can."

That week was hectic for Pippa. She raced out to Jeremy's every night, arriving breathless and keyed up with anticipation. Sometimes they went out to dinner at little places along the coast where they could hold hands unashamedly. Other times they ate at home, restraining themselves under the disinterested, yet restrictive eye of Mrs. Dunphy. In a way, that was fun too. It made their lovemaking that much more exciting for having to be delayed.

Pippa was blissful, but Jeremy was dissatisfied. "I want to take you to the finest places in Los Angeles and show you off," he complained.

"I know, darling," Pippa soothed. She grinned suddenly. "I wouldn't mind displaying my catch either, but you can't have everything."

"The hell with all of them! Tomorrow night we're getting dressed up and doing the town. We'll go to Ma Maison," he decided. "I understand it's so exclusive they have an unlisted phone number."

Pippa blanched, hoping the candlelight would hide it. She had interviewed a number of the regulars at that posh restaurant. "It sounds tacky to me. Why would you want to go to a place that Hollywood?"

"I don't really," he smiled ruefully. "I just thought you would." Jeremy's smile faded. "I don't want this thing between us to be hole in the corner, Pippa. Our relationship is too beautiful for that."

She was touched. "I agree, Jeremy, that's why I want to keep it private. Once people got their hands on it, things would never be the same."

He sighed. "I suppose you're right, but I still feel you're getting the short end of the stick."

She gave him a melting smile. "Then why don't you make it up to me tonight?"

Much later, when they were lying in each other's arms, Jeremy returned to the subject. "I feel this is so wrong, Pippa, hiding you away. Won't you let me take you to the kind of places you deserve?"

She curled her arm around his neck, kissing his throat. "Neither of us likes those phony restaurants and clubs, suppose we make a deal. We'll go to Knott's Berry Farm on Saturday." She would wangle the time off somehow.

He raised an eyebrow. "A farm?"

"Like none you've ever been to," she promised.

The proposed outing presented her with a dilemma. Schedules in the newsroom were rotated periodically so no one had to work every weekend. The trouble was that Pippa had drawn Saturday and Sunday duty that month. Juggling her days and hours so Jeremy wouldn't suspect anything was getting a little complicated.

Woody was a continuing pain also. He hung around her desk, making even more of a nuisance of himself than ever, but Pippa didn't let that bother her. The bet had long ceased to be of any importance to her, although not to Woody.

"I should have put a time limit on this thing," he grumbled.

"That's your trouble, Woody," Pippa needled. "You can't think of more than one thing at a time."

"You're awfully cocky for someone who has yet to deliver the goods," he remarked sourly.

Pippa's high spirits were a worry to Woody. In spite of the lack of results so far, was she really onto something?

"I'm not in any hurry." She gave him an elfin grin. "It's too much fun watching you agonize."

"It's the *last* laugh that counts," he warned.

"Not necessarily. You've provided me with more than fifty dollars worth of amusement already."

He was quick to pounce on that. "So I was right! You're not getting anywhere."

The memory of those nights in Jeremy's arms gave a soft glow to her face. "I wouldn't say that," she murmured.

"I hear Hawke moved out of the Beverly Wilshire," Woody said abruptly. "Would you know why?"

Pippa shrugged. "Maybe the beds were too hard."

Woody's grin was lecherous. "That sounds like first-hand knowledge."

She forced down the anger that flared swiftly. Woody had a knack of making something beautiful sound ugly. Pippa regarded him steadily. "Your deductive reasoning is about on a par with your writing. If I were sleeping with the man, would I have any trouble getting an interview?"

She was rewarded by the frustration on his face, but Pippa felt a shiver of apprehension. Woody must never discover the truth. He couldn't begin to comprehend the love she felt for Jeremy, or the affection Jeremy felt for her. It wasn't a tawdry affair between them. Even though Jeremy didn't love her, he *cared*. It was evident in the tenderness of his lovemaking. Nothing could ever come of it because of her fatal deception, but Pippa would cherish the memory of him for the rest of her life. Woody mustn't be allowed to tarnish their precious relationship.

Pippa stood up abruptly, unwilling to fence with him anymore. Someday she would tell Woody exactly what she thought of him—in words of one syllable so he'd understand—but not now.

Pippa managed to change her schedule so she could have that Saturday off, but as they drove to Anaheim she tried to explain to Jeremy that she couldn't see him the next day. He didn't take it well.

"It's Sunday!" he complained. "I was looking forward to seeing you in the daylight."

"It won't be any different tomorrow," she pointed out.

"You know what I mean. Our days together are so limited."

"Thank heaven the nights are plentiful," she teased. Pippa put her hand on his thigh, tracing the taut muscles she had come to know so well.

His big hand covered her caressing fingers. "A little more of that and I'll pull over to the side of the road and have my way with you, woman."

"Promises, promises," she mocked. As Jeremy steered into the right-hand lane, Pippa gasped, "I was only joking!"

"Be forewarned; I never joke about making love. It's serious business."

She fluttered her eyelashes at him. "That's what I like, a man who's devoted to his work."

Tiny embers made Jeremy's green eyes glow like a predatory cat's. "With very little encouragement I'd turn around and head for home."

"No, we're almost there, and I do want you to see Knott's Berry Farm," she answered reluctantly.

"You mean I can't compete with a bunch of cows and chickens? I must really be losing my grip."

"I'll reassure you later," she promised.

Knott's Berry Farm had indeed started out as that, with a roadside stand that sold the boysenberries they grew. In time, the family added a small lunchroom, serving fried chicken, also home grown. As the fame of its cooking spread they enlarged the restaurant, but people still had to wait a long time to get seated. To keep them amused an old time Western village was added, complete with saloon, jail, and dry goods emporium. Costumed characters wandered the unpaved streets, staging impromptu shootouts for the bemused visitors.

The place had grown into a huge amusement park, but Pippa steered Jeremy to the old section, remembering her own delight in it.

He was fascinated, as she had hoped he would be. "Why haven't I ever heard about this place?"

"Because you spend all your time going to snooty restaurants," she informed him.

"Only because I'm underprivileged," he laughed.

"No, because you're rich." Suddenly Pippa needed reassurance. "Are you really enjoying yourself, Jeremy?"

His eyes were an intangible caress. "Can you doubt it?"

On the way home, replete with fried chicken, biscuits, and boysenberry pie, he sighed happily. "That beats coq au vin any day."

Pippa's head was resting on the back of the seat. She turned to smile at him. "Stick with me, kid. I'll show you how the other half lives."

He frowned. "You seem to have gotten the impression that I'm accustomed to having a footman behind every chair."

"Not exactly, but you must admit not many of us keep horses on our twelve acres."

"All right, I've been luckier than most people, but I've worked for it."

"Knowing you, I don't doubt it for a minute," Pippa said softly. "Tell me how you became such a success, Jeremy."

"I was always fascinated by computers," he said slowly. "They're such wonderfully complex things. Do you realize we couldn't have put a man on the moon without them?"

"I've always heard that. But, like many people, I object to a machine being smarter than I am."

"A lot of people feel that way." He lifted her hand, placing a kiss in the palm. "Don't worry, my love, you'll never be replaced by a machine."

"That's very comforting." Pippa's fingers curled to retain the impression of his mouth. "But you still haven't told me how you got started."

He shrugged. "The whole concept was pretty much in its infancy when I got out of college, which made it all the more exciting. I started a small company that grew into a big one." He made light of his success. "In those days you could hardly lose."

Pippa knew that wasn't true of any business. Jeremy was simply one of life's winners. "Have you ever had a problem you couldn't solve?" she asked curiously.

Jeremy's face was suddenly austere as he stared out the windshield. "Funny you should ask that."

She was smitten by remorse, knowing what was troubling him. "If you're worried about me, don't be, Jeremy. I went into this knowing the score."

He turned his head to stare at her for a moment. "Which is?"

"We're both adults," she explained carefully. "We know what we're doing, and we're not hurting anyone."

A vein throbbed at his temple. "I wish I could share your confidence."

"This won't change your life," she said urgently. "In years to come, I hope you'll remember me with joy, not regret." She bowed her head suddenly. "Just remember me, Jeremy."

His hand crushed hers in a painful grip. "I wish I could be as sure of everything in this world."

Pippa took a deep breath, pushing the sadness behind her. There would be plenty of time for tears when Jeremy went out of her life. "It must be the fried chicken that's weighing us down. We need some exercise. How about a moonlight swim before I go home?"

"Stay with me tonight, Pippa," he urged.

"I can't," she declined regretfully.

"Then I'll stay at your place."

"No, it . . . my aunt might take it into her head to come over early." It was the excuse she had given for not being with him, a visiting aunt from out of town.

Jeremy pulled into the carport of the Malibu house. "Don't go, Pippa. For some reason I have this terrible feeling of impending disaster." His arms closed tightly around her as he buried his face in her hair. "I want to keep you safely by my side."

Pippa slipped her arms around his waist inside his

jacket, trailing her fingers down his spine to slip inside his waistband. "I guarantee nothing's going to happen for the next couple of hours," she whispered. "If I forego the swim, can you think of something else to keep me amused?"

Sunday was definitely not a day to be cooped up in the newsroom. Pippa's wistful gaze kept returning to the bright sunshine outside. She wondered what Jeremy was doing. Was he sunbathing on the deck after an early morning swim? She could just picture that virile male body relaxed in a lounger, his dark head upturned to catch the warmth of the sun.

It was an effort not to reach for the phone and call him, but Pippa restrained herself. The sound of typewriters and wire-service equipment would be hard to explain. Sighing deeply, she went back to work.

Pippa had told Jeremy she was going to spend both the day and night with her aunt, intending to use the evening doing accumulated chores. Between working and spending all her free time with Jeremy, she hadn't had a moment to wash clothes or clean the apartment.

As the clock inched toward seven, she changed her mind. Why should she waste time on mundane things when their hours together were so limited? She would drive down to Malibu and surprise Jeremy, Pippa decided. She smiled happily, anticipating his delight.

As she pulled up to the lovely beach house a little later, Pippa experienced a warm feeling of coming home. She ran up the walk, flinging open the door and calling his name. When there was no answer she felt a tremendous letdown. It hadn't even occurred to her that Jeremy might not be home. Why hadn't she called and told him she was coming?

The silvery sound of a woman's laughter brought Pippa's head up sharply.

She walked slowly into the living room, feeling a cold little knot forming in the pit of her stomach. Through the wide glass windows Pippa saw Jeremy bending over a woman lying on a deck chair. It was a tableau that would remain forever frozen in her memory. Jeremy had on a warm-up jacket over brief navy trunks that rode low on his narrow hips. The deep tan of his hand next to her face contrasted sharply with the pale skin of the blond woman smiling up at him.

Pippa remained rooted to the spot, as motionless as the couple she was staring at. Then there was a puff of smoke from the woman's cigarette as Jeremy straightened up and tossed a match in the ashtray.

Pippa came out of her trance, a roaring in her ears from the rush of blood to her head. Yes, she should certainly have called ahead! What a fool she had been to think Jeremy was languishing here alone. Almost as great a fool as to think what they had together was something special, Pippa decided bitterly.

Tears misted her eyes as she turned to leave, intent only on getting out of there. In her haste she stumbled against a small table, sending an ornament clattering to the polished floor. Jeremy looked through the window, seeing her for the first time. A wealth of emotions coursed over his face as he strode to the door.

"Pippa! I didn't expect you."

She gave him an acrid smile. "That's pretty obvious."

"Listen to me," he said urgently. "Don't be—"

"You must be Pippa." The tall blond woman joined them. "I'd know you anywhere from Jeremy's description. I'm Calla Robertson." She extended her hand with a charming smile.

Pippa stared at her in despair. Calla was everything she had feared. The beautiful, serene face framed by shining blond hair was as near perfection as the slim, curved body. She was somewhere around thirty, mature and confident.

While Jeremy was making the introductions, Calla was subjecting Pippa to the same frank appraisal. "I'm so glad I got to meet you," she said.

"I—I didn't mean to barge in," Pippa blurted out, her normal poise deserting her.

"It's an unexpected pleasure," Calla assured her, even managing to make it sound like she meant it. "Do stay and have dinner with us."

"No, I couldn't," Pippa gasped. "I just stopped by to . . . I think I left my sunglasses when we were all swimming here the other day. I have to get back."

"Well, at least you have time for a drink," the other woman coaxed. "Convince her, Jeremy."

His face was impassive. "That's difficult to do once Pippa makes up her mind."

Pippa's simmering anger sprang into full blaze. She knew he was challenging her, not answering Calla's request. He didn't even have the grace to be embarrassed at being caught!

Pippa lifted her chin, ignoring Jeremy as she addressed herself to the other woman. "After being separated for so long, I'm sure you two have a lot to talk about."

"We've already done that." Calla and Jeremy exchanged a look that Pippa couldn't decipher. It wasn't the secret glance that lovers exchange, yet there was some kind of understanding in it. Calla turned back to Pippa. "Now I'd like to get to know you. Jeremy made you sound very interesting. I have a feeling we're going to be good friends."

Pippa realized that under different circumstances it would have been true. All her preconceived notions had proved false. Calla was the kind of woman she admired, warm and direct, with no silly female game-playing. It made Jeremy's double-dealing even more despicable.

She managed to respond to Calla's remark calmly. "I'm sure we would, but I don't get to San Francisco often."

"You can never tell. Life is full of surprises," the other woman answered gently.

Didn't she know it! Pippa stood up with determination. "I really must be going. It was so nice meeting you." She drew herself up to her full height, facing Jeremy rigidly. "Next time I won't drop in unannounced. Although, come to think of it, you needn't worry—there won't be a next time."

His face was expressionless. "I'll see you to your car."

"That isn't necessary. I might not seem too bright at times, but I can find my way outside without assistance."

With a muttered exclamation of annoyance Jeremy seized her upper arm in a painful grip, hustling Pippa toward the door.

As soon as they were out of Calla's sight she jerked her arm away, whipping around to face him furiously. "Take your hands off me! I don't ever want you to touch me again."

He grasped her shoulders, his fingers biting into her tender skin. "Will you kindly let me explain?"

"What is there to explain? That it completely slipped your mind that your girlfriend was coming?"

"Of course not, I—"

"When were you planning to tell me?" Her eyes spit dislike at him. "Or was it going to be your little secret? Maybe you were planning to alternate between my place and yours."

He shook her until her soft hair flew into disarray around her flushed face. "I ought to put you over my knee and whale the tar out of you for that!"

"Don't try it, buster," she snapped. "And it's one of the nicer things I could have said to you."

Her hard push on his chest caught him off balance. Before he could recover, Pippa raced to her car, slamming the door and locking it. Jeremy was after her in a flash, rapping on the closed window.

"There are a few things I have to say to you, young woman," he declared grimly.

"Write me a letter," she advised, racing the motor and backing out of the driveway.

Pippa rolled down the windows once she was on the highway, letting the fresh air cool her hot cheeks. But nothing could quench her fiery anger or dull the terrible pain that sliced through her. How could Jeremy have been so devious?

113

Pippa had always known she was just an interlude in his life, but she'd thought it was an idyllic one, a precious space of time that would forever be enshrined in both their hearts. It was agonizing to realize that for him it was just another affair. Not even a completely satisfying one if he had to send for another woman.

Pippa's hands gripped the steering wheel until her fingers ached, remembering those nights in Jeremy's arms. Could all of that tenderness, all that consideration, be contrived? Merely the mechanical actions of a consummate lover? Surely not!

Even as she denied it, Pippa told herself not to be a fool. Jeremy was a virile man who needed a woman; she had just happened to be the one. He wasn't any different from any other man.

She set her chin grimly, staring at the white line in the road. It was a bitter lesson, but she'd get over it. Just as she would get over Jeremy Hawke.

CHAPTER SEVEN

Pippa went into the newsroom early the next morning since she couldn't sleep anyway. She had stayed in bed until the sky started to pale, giving up about six o'clock.

After showering and donning a pair of jeans and a plaid shirt, Pippa brushed her golden brown hair until it crackled. It was a way of venting her frustration. She hadn't intended to put on any makeup, until the mirror showed her the ravages Jeremy had wrought. But no more! With a determined hand she erased the circles under her eyes and put a blush of color on each pale cheek. It was a bright badge of courage, a declaration of her independence. She was in charge of her own life, not dependent on anyone for her well-being—least of all Jeremy Hawke.

The only thing she couldn't replace was the sparkle that was missing from her eyes. Would it ever return? Would life ever seem full and exciting again? With a frown of annoyance Pippa closed the front door decisively.

At that exact moment the phone began to ring. Her slender body stiffened. Could it be Jeremy? She was furious with herself at the sudden hope that jolted her. Gritting her teeth, Pippa continued on to her car.

In the unaccustomed early morning quiet, Pippa got a lot of work done. She dug out several human interest stories that had been awaiting the right moment, getting involved in other people's lives in an attempt to forget her own.

People drifted in without disturbing her concentration. Only Woody failed to respect her creativity. He showed up long after the others, zeroing in on Pippa immediately.

"I'm surprised to see *you* here," he leered. "I thought you'd be playing on the beach."

Pippa's hands stilled on the typewriter keys. That meant Woody had finally discovered Jeremy's whereabouts. Well, what difference did it make? It no longer mattered if Jeremy found out the truth about her. Their opinion of each other would merely match.

"No answer, Pippa? I never knew you to be at a loss for words," Woody taunted.

"Too bad I can't say the same for you," she replied automatically.

"It kind of shakes you up to find I'm gaining on you, doesn't it?"

"You couldn't catch up with me if I left a trail of bread crumbs," she told him disgustedly.

He reddened angrily. "So you got there first, big deal. Where did it get you?"

"I could ask you the same thing."

Woody's face took on a crafty expression. "I'm working on it."

"That must be a new experience for you," she needled.

"Go ahead and have a good laugh. You're going to need it." His manner bore a certain air of assurance. "Times have changed, kid. I'm the one with the inside track now."

"You've spoken to Hawke?" Pippa asked warily. Surely Jeremy would have mentioned it to her. Then she realized there was no reason why he should.

"Does Macy's tell Gimbels?" Woody asked airily. He turned his head to look over his shoulder at Gloria. "Get me a cup of coffee," he ordered.

Pippa stilled the rush of anger that rose immediately.

116

Narrowing her eyes, she drawled, "Isn't that a little blatant even for you, Woody?"

He didn't back down. "What's wrong with the junior writer getting the senior one a cup of coffee?"

"I don't have time to tell you all the reasons." Pippa exchanged a glance with Gloria. "There's an open box of rat poison in the kitchen. Be sure you don't use it instead of sugar—that stuff is expensive."

Woody's face darkened. "Just wait," he muttered, wheeling around and starting for the door to the courtyard.

At the briefing meeting a little later, Pippa requested the assignment to cover a labor dispute in Long Beach, about thirty miles from Los Angeles.

"They're taking a vote this afternoon, but the result is anybody's guess," she remarked. "If they do go on strike, I'll send for a camera crew."

"I don't know, Pippa." Ray hesitated. "Those waterfront disputes can get pretty ugly."

She nodded. "A strike would close down the docks and cripple the shipping industry."

"Tempers run pretty high," Ray noted. "Maybe it would be better to send—" he stopped abruptly.

Pippa knew exactly what was going through his mind. Maybe we'd better send a man. It was the kind of thinking that infuriated her. Ray was better than most bosses, but even he had an occasional blind spot. Pippa didn't intend to allow him to get away with it, however. She was the top reporter at KCTV, and this was a big story.

If Woody had wanted it, they might have had to battle it out on the basis of seniority, but Pippa knew he wouldn't touch it with a stick. The assignment meant hanging around the labor hall most of the night if the vote was delayed, then having to be back at the crack of dawn in case something broke early. Meals consisted of fast food brought in from the nearest chain. It was too much like work for Woody.

Pippa looked steadily at Ray. "I think you know I'm capable of handling it."

In the late afternoon Pippa stopped by her apartment to pack a bag, just in case. Ray had given in reluctantly, as she knew he must. He realized that she wouldn't let the matter rest, and he had no reason except sexism to refuse her. To his credit, Pippa understood that he was concerned about her safety, not her ability. It didn't delight her though. When would men realize it was time to do away with the double standard?

The treatment she received in Long Beach was balm to Pippa's ruffled sensibilities. She was greeted from all sides in the common newsroom set up for the media. Pippa was popular with her colleagues—both men and women —because of her professionalism, and the fact that she didn't trade on her femininity.

She exchanged industry gossip with the people she hadn't seen recently, drinking numerous cups of coffee and forgetting her problems in the pleasure of being with her peers.

When the vote was postponed endlessly, as they had all feared, Pippa joined a poker game in progress.

Mac Gunther, the correspondent from the *Times,* moved over to make room for her. "Thank God they sent you instead of Phelan."

"What's the matter, Mac, did Woody take your money last time?" Pippa grinned.

"That guy couldn't take an aspirin," he told her disgustedly. "I just can't stand him, that's all."

"He could give the ministry a bad name," Walt Jacobsen agreed. He was a reporter for a rival station. "Remember that tragedy where the woman lost her three kids in a fire? Phelan actually asked her if she planned to have more children!"

Pippa sighed. "He's not exactly Mr. Sensitive, is he?"

Mac's mouth turned down at the corners. "He ought to be working on one of those tabloid rags where he could use his only two talents—bribery and blackmail."

"Are we going to play poker, or are we going to talk

about that creep all night?" one of the other men complained.

It was two in the morning before a representative of the union came to tell them that the vote had been postponed until the next day.

"Well, another day, another hotel room." Walt stood up and stretched. "You want to share it with me, Pippa?" He gave her a mock leer.

"Sure, as soon as you bring a note from your wife saying it's okay," she smiled.

"What's this prejudice you have against married men?" he asked plaintively.

"Did you ever think maybe you just don't turn her on?" Mac joked. "A foxy lady like Pippa can have her pick of the litter. What would she want with an old dog like you?"

"I was a boy scout," Walt offered hopefully. "I'm honest, clean, and brave."

"I notice you left out faithful," Pippa remarked dryly.

That was something she had found out the hard way— that *no* man was. As they all drifted off to their hotel rooms, a black depression settled over her. Why did they have to remind her of Jeremy? For a short space of time she had felt like her old self. Would he always sneak back like a thief to rob her life of zest? With a groan Pippa buried her head under the pillow.

The next day was a replay of the one before. The assembled reporters took it in stride, not really expecting anything else. There was an element of show business in the proceedings. Neither side wanted to trivialize the situation by coming to a hasty decision. The cynical media settled in, ready for whatever happened.

It was afternoon. They were all resigned to another night in a hotel when the news came down. There would be no strike.

"My wife is going to take this as a mixed blessing," Walt grinned. "She'll have to cook dinner for me now."

"Why don't you be a sport and take her out to dinner?" Pippa suggested.

"She'd think I had a guilty conscience," he laughed. "See you around, Pippa."

It was after five when Pippa reached Los Angeles. She had phoned in her story and would have been forgiven for going home, but there was nothing to go home for. She decided to return to the newsroom.

"We didn't expect you back," Gloria greeted her.

"Well, I thought I'd check in and see what's doing."

"It must have been very exciting down there where all the action was." Gloria's expression was one of admiration.

"There wasn't much action because the strike was averted at the last minute, but it was fun," Pippa admitted. "Too bad it didn't last."

Gloria looked at her friend's drooping mouth. "Is anything wrong, Pippa?"

"No, everything's nifty." Pippa pinned a determined smile on her face.

Gloria wasn't fooled. "Is there anything I can do?" she asked softly.

"I'm just a little tired and a lot hungry," Pippa insisted. "That junk food doesn't stay with you."

"Why don't you come home and have dinner with Scott and me?"

"After working all day, you don't need company."

"You're not company. Besides, I plan to put you to work. Scott is always too busy studying to dry the dishes for me."

It didn't take any more urging on Gloria's part. Pippa hadn't realized how much she was dreading going back to her empty apartment. Almost since she met Jeremy, they had spent all their free hours together. Pippa hadn't had the time or the desire to see anyone else. Suddenly it had come to a screeching halt, leaving an aching void.

Scott greeted her fondly with a kiss on the cheek. "It's good to see you, Pippa. Where have you been keeping yourself? We haven't seen you in ages."

"You know how it is," she answered vaguely.

"Has some tall, dark Superman been taking up all your time?" he teased.

"Don't I wish," she answered shortly. Pippa changed the subject. "How's school, Scott?"

"Tough, but I'll make it." He regarded his wife lovingly. "I have to after all Gloria's doing to put me through."

They were sitting in the kitchen, watching Gloria bustle around the small room. She paused in her labors, returning his look with one of such adoration that Pippa felt like an interloper. The brief moment passed as Gloria resumed washing the lettuce.

"Just remember who you belong to when those gorgeous co-eds try to hit on you," she laughed.

"You have nothing to worry about, my love. I wouldn't touch them with asbestos gloves," Scott declared.

"That's what they all say, isn't it, Pippa?" Gloria tried to enlist her friend's support.

"You're asking the wrong one." Pippa managed a smile. "I'm no authority on men."

"No, I mean it," Scott insisted. He grinned suddenly. "Now, if Pippa gave me a tumble it would be a different story. There's no challenge with those young kids. Some of them fall into bed with a guy they just met. Who'd want a girl like that?"

A spoon clattered out of Gloria's hand. Her face was very pale as she bent to pick it up.

"You can't indict all kids," Pippa said casually. "Sometimes they just make foolish mistakes. Living with it would be hard enough without having people sit in judgment."

"You mean like falling for a smooth line, or being stupid enough to drown their inhibitions in a highball glass?" Scott asked scornfully. "I don't buy that."

"It takes two to tango," Pippa reminded him succinctly. "Save some of your condemnation for your own sex."

"Dinner's ready," Gloria said in a strangled voice.

During dinner the slight unpleasantness was glossed

over. By the time they took their coffee into the living room, it was forgotten.

"Don't be such a stranger." Scott kissed Pippa's cheek before going off to study. "We miss you when you're not around."

"Is tomorrow night too soon?" she teased.

While they were doing the dishes, Gloria turned a misery-filled face to Pippa. "Now do you see why I'm such a wreck? If Scott ever found out about Woody, he'd leave me."

"You don't really believe that!"

"You heard him." Gloria blinked her long eyelashes rapidly

"People say things without thinking about them very deeply when they're just talking abstractly," Pippa assured her.

"I wouldn't want to put it to the test," Gloria answered forlornly.

"There's no reason why you should. It was an isolated incident that happened long before you met Scott."

"I might not have any choice. Just lately Woody's been worse than ever. He was a little better after you declared war, but now he's reverted." Gloria bit her lip, giving Pippa a worried look. "I'm afraid you made a terrible enemy when you forced him to back down in front of the whole newsroom."

Pippa shrugged. "Look at it this way: There are only two kinds of people, friends and enemies. I sure don't want Woody for a friend, so what's left?"

A smile lightened Gloria's troubled expression. "You might not have good sense, but nobody can fault you on loyalty." Her smile died. "I don't know, Pip. It's almost like he knows something we don't, and is plotting to use it against both of us."

"You worry too much. There's nothing he can do to me, and I'm sure he knows I wouldn't let it pass if he tried anything with you."

"I hope you're right." Gloria didn't sound convinced.

"Cheer up, at least you'll have a few days respite. We

all will. It's time for Woody's annual ego trip to Sacramento."

Pippa worried over Gloria on the way home. In spite of her reassurances, she was afraid Woody might actually try to break up Gloria's marriage. Whether he could accomplish it or not was another thing, but he was rotten enough to try. Would Scott react as Gloria feared? Somehow Pippa didn't think so. He was a thoroughly nice person and there was no doubt about his deep love for Gloria. It was like Woody to want to flaw something beautiful.

Pippa's apartment seemed even more bleak after the love and laughter at the Cullens'. After turning on all the lights she switched on the stereo. It was still only an empty collection of rooms. She was just tired, she decided. It had been a hard two days. What she needed was a hot bath and some sleep.

She washed her hair in the shower, blowing it dry afterward. It fell in a glorious mass of gold-tipped waves about her bare shoulders, but Pippa regarded it indifferently. She had just slipped into a lace-trimmed, yellow chiffon nightgown when the doorbell rang. Her eyes went to the clock on the nightstand. Ten thirty. Who could it be at this hour?

The bell rang again in a strident blast, as though someone were holding a finger on the button. As Pippa ran to the door in alarm, the bell was replaced by a loud pounding on the panels.

"I know you're in there; I can see the lights. Open this door, Pippa!" Jeremy's voice demanded.

"Are you out of your mind? You'll wake the whole neighborhood," she cried.

"Their sleeping habits don't interest me." His voice was only slightly muffled.

"Go away! I never want to see you again," she declared dramatically.

"That's unfortunate, because you're going to." He

sounded grimly determined. "We have some things to straighten out."

"I'm not interested in anything you have to say."

"Perhaps the neighbors are. I saw a few lights go on."

Pippa suddenly realized that the whole building was about to become privy to her personal life. Yanking the door open, she confronted Jeremy furiously. "Get in here this minute!"

He paused on the threshold, the harsh lines of his face softening as he looked at the cloud of silky hair surrounding her small, flushed face. A rush of emotions played across his mobile features.

Pippa was too distracted to notice. Her own emotions were giving her trouble. Jeremy's sudden appearance hadn't given her time to prepare herself. As they stared into each other's eyes, a spreading warmth invaded Pippa's midsection. In the space of that one split-second, her body remembered all the things her mind was trying to forget.

She refused to let the spell envelop her. "I suppose you know this is blackmail."

Jeremy recovered too, a frown drawing his peaked brows together. "Where the hell have you been for two days?"

His authoritative manner made her answer without thinking. "I went to Long Beach to—" Pippa stopped abruptly. "What business is it of yours?"

His frown deepened into a scowl as he advanced on her. "Were you with a man?"

She flung her head back. "I was with a lot of men, as it happens."

His hands bit into her bare shoulders. "If I believed that, I'd kill you!"

In spite of her sense of outrage, Pippa was a little frightened by the black rage on his face. "Let go of me," she cried breathlessly. "What right do you have to barge in here and threaten me?"

He ignored that completely, jerking her savagely toward him. "Answer my question! Did you go away with a man?"

"No!" The truth was torn out of her. "I just . . . I wanted to get away for a while." Since Jeremy didn't seem to know the truth about her, Pippa didn't think this was the time to tell him.

His punishing grip on her shoulders relaxed. "I've been going out of my mind since you left Sunday night," he groaned. "I phoned the next morning and I've been calling day and night ever since. Tonight I finally decided to come over and camp on your doorstep until you showed up."

Pippa was unimpressed. "What's the matter, did you have a fight with Calla?"

"That's what I wanted to talk to you about, Pippa."

She turned away, wrapping her arms around her trembling body. "It isn't necessary. I saw the complete picture for myself."

"I didn't expect her," Jeremy said quietly. "Calla arrived Sunday morning—to surprise me, she said." His mouth twisted wryly.

Pippa faced him with eyes like blazing sapphires. "Does that make it any better? She must have been pretty sure of her welcome if she arrived bag and baggage. Either way, you're a two-timing rat! How could you have made love to me, even asked me to move in with you, when you were in love with another woman?" To her dismay, Pippa heard tears thickening her voice.

"I was never in love with Calla. We've been friends for many years." At Pippa's derisive snort he said, "All right, so maybe our relationship went a little further than that, but there was never any commitment."

"I'll bet Calla thought differently," Pippa remarked bitterly.

"Not really. She was just feeling lonely and nostalgic. Calla doesn't love me either. We talked it all out. I put her on a plane Monday morning."

"You shouldn't have done that," Pippa maintained, determined not to let this man manipulate her again.

125

"You're going to get very lonesome in that big house all by yourself."

His hands were at her waist, drawing her gently closer. "Am I going to be alone, Pippa?"

She held him off. "I suppose not. You can have your pick of women in this town."

"You know that's not what I meant." His low voice was caressing her.

She pulled away, turning her back on him. "It wouldn't work, Jeremy. Now that I've seen Calla, I realize how wrong you and I are for each other. Besides being a nice person, she's what you want in a woman—everything I'm not."

His arms went around Pippa's waist, drawing her against his hard length. "Tell me what I want in a woman," he chuckled.

Her hands locked around his muscular forearms, trying to break his tantalizing embrace. "Someone cool, and serene, and compliant."

Jeremy nuzzled her soft hair aside so he could nibble on her earlobe. "And you're fiery, excitable, and independent."

"Exactly," she gasped, raising her shoulder to dislodge his disturbing mouth.

"I guess I'll just have to learn to live with it," he laughed.

Pippa became very still in his arms. What was he saying?

Jeremy took the opportunity to turn her toward him. His hands trailed down her back to mold her hips to his. "Do you know the hell I've been going through," he groaned, "missing you, wanting you."

She could feel his hardened loins through the thin scrap of chiffon separating them. Pippa's legs started to tremble, her will to resist this man deserting her rapidly. "Let me go, Jeremy, *please!*"

He ignored the desperate plea. His warm mouth slid down her neck to her shoulders and then to the curve of her breast, tantalizing her with the promise of rapture she knew he could bring.

When he searched out the taut nipple under the film of lace, rolling it between his lips, Pippa gave up the struggle. This was the man she loved, miraculously returned to her after she had thought she would never see him again. How could she deny the need that was turning her liquid inside?

"Did you really miss me?" she whispered.

"I'll show you how much," he muttered.

His mouth closed urgently over hers in a kiss so demanding that she was shaken by it. His tongue probed deeply, staking a claim that was unmistakably masculine. Pippa gloried in this evidence of his passion, raking her fingers through his thick hair and murmuring his name repeatedly.

When Jeremy finally dragged his mouth from hers, his breathing was labored. "How could you have done it, darling? How could you run off and leave me like that?"

She struggled to catch her own breath, smoothing his eyebrows with loving fingers. "You would have done the same thing if you'd come in unexpectedly and found me with another man," she protested.

He laughed triumphantly, sweeping her up in his arms and carrying her to the couch. "Don't you believe it! I'd have taken him by the scruff of the neck and the seat of his pants and thrown him out bodily."

She looked up at him through long lashes. "And what would you have done to me?"

Jeremy's eyes darkened as he bent her back against the pillows. "You know exactly what I would have done to you, my lovely little enchantress." His hand cupped around her breast as his mouth feathered scorching kisses on her delicate skin.

A shudder ran through Pippa. "Oh, Jeremy, if you only knew the things I was imagining."

He slipped the nightgown off her shoulders, feasting his eyes on a pink-tipped mound. His lips touched it tenderly. "Were you remembering this, sweetheart?"

Her hands restlessly caressed the strong column of his neck. "No, I was picturing you and . . ." She couldn't go on.

There was raw desire in Jeremy's eyes as he raised his head to stare down at her. "How could you think I'd want any other woman when I have you?"

The ring of sincerity in his voice was as unmistakable as the hard thrust of his body against hers. Pippa gazed up at him provocatively. "Didn't you mention something about showing me?"

Jeremy stretched out on the couch next to her, turning Pippa so that her body was arched against him. His hand stroked her hip, then wandered under the hem of her gown to caress the smooth contour of her inner thigh. "Are you convinced?" he muttered thickly.

She gave him a lazy smile, slowly unbuttoning his shirt. "I'm beginning to be," she murmured, one finger tracing the curling hair on his chest down to his navel.

Without taking his eyes from hers, Jeremy pulled his shirt out of his slacks, shrugging it off his broad shoulders. Pippa unbuckled his belt, a slight tremor going through her as he completed the job.

He left her for only a moment while he took off the rest of his clothes, returning to draw her nightgown over her head. When she was naked in his arms, feeling the pulsing desire that gripped him, Jeremy smiled down at her. "I'm about to settle any remaining doubts."

Their delight in each other was intensified by the recent misunderstanding. Both sought to give pleasure, succeeding beyond their wildest dreams. Jeremy's hands and mouth brought Pippa to heights she had never reached before, as he used all of his secret knowledge of her body and its pleasure spots.

Their ultimate union was breathtaking, a driving force that carried them through an inferno. They emerged in a shower of sparks that died down gradually. Pippa felt peace spreading through her as she made the slow spiral back to earth in Jeremy's arms. They fell asleep that way.

It was a long time later that Pippa awoke to find him still clasping her close. Her heart swelled with love as she looked down at his strong face, the firm mouth still curved in a little smile.

There were no longer any doubts in her mind. It didn't matter what other women there had been in his life. The important thing was that Jeremy belonged to *her*.

Sometime after their passionate lovemaking, Pippa had had a revelation. Jeremy was in love with her! He might not know it yet, or maybe he was fighting against the idea, but it was true. They were bound together by a bond too strong to break, no matter what his reservations.

The road ahead was fraught with obstacles though. For one thing, there was that terribly dangerous deception of hers to clear up. That had to be done as soon as possible, and in a way that wouldn't injure his male pride. Then she had to gently implant the idea of marriage; nothing but complete possession was going to satisfy Pippa.

It wasn't going to be easy to get a bridle on this wild stallion, but it could be done. Pippa looked down at her sleeping giant, smiling tenderly.

CHAPTER EIGHT

Pippa was a changed woman when she got to the newsroom the next day. The defensive thrust of her shoulders was gone and there was a new softness to her face.

Gloria noticed it immediately. "I must be a better cook than I thought. That dinner last night sure cleared up what ailed you."

"Nothing like a little help from my friends," Pippa agreed with sparkling eyes. "You look pretty chipper yourself."

"It's only a temporary condition in my case, I'm afraid, but I'm not complaining. Woody has gone to the writer's conference," Gloria explained.

"Keep a good thought," Pippa advised. "Maybe he won't be able to find his way home."

It was late afternoon when Ray came out of his office with a face like a thundercloud. He was usually so even-tempered that Pippa looked at him curiously. "What's up, Ray? You look as though you'd like to kick the cat."

"I'd like to kick Woody!" the producer exploded. "Do you know what that idiot's done? Merely gone off to Sacramento without turning in the finished copy on abuses in local nursing homes. It's the lead story in the B segment tonight."

"I thought he was off today."

"I made him write it yesterday before he left. It's his

130

story and I see no reason to sit on it until he comes back from strewing his words of dubious wisdom." Ray swore pungently under his breath. "I've never been able to understand how that could take three days."

Pippa's eyebrows climbed. Ray had never been as explicit about his feelings before. If that's the way he felt, why didn't he fire the creep? Pippa thought she knew the answer to that. She had always suspected that Woody was protected by people in higher places, and this seemed to prove it. Woody was a toady who knew the right boots to lick.

"Get on the phone and have him read it back to you, Pippa," Ray ordered disgustedly.

Why me? she wanted to ask. Instead she glanced at the clock. "What if he's not there yet?"

"He will be," Ray answered curtly. "There's an indoctrination luncheon for all the lecturers. Woody wouldn't miss it. It's complimentary, but he puts it on his expense account."

So Ray knew about Woody's little self-instigated fringe benefits, Pippa reflected thoughtfully. "Do you know where he's staying?"

"At the best hotel. Where else?" he asked sardonically.

Pippa dialed the number, wishing she hadn't been elected to the job. She changed her mind after the room clerk told her Woody wasn't registered. It took a few more phone calls to track down the rest of the story.

"Mr. Phelan hasn't been with us for the last two years," the head of the conference told her. "We were sorry to lose him, but I understand that nothing is forever."

"You're quite right, Mr. Brightbart," she told the man. "I think Woody's time is running out." After she hung up the phone Pippa stared at it thoughtfully for a long moment before picking it up and dialing again.

"Yeah, who is it?" Woody sounded annoyed. There was soft music playing in the background.

"How nice to find you home," Pippa said sweetly.

131

"And all day today I was picturing you as a father-figure to all the young tyros in Sacramento."

There was a pulsing silence on the other end before Woody said, "I got hung up here finishing some work. As a matter of fact, you just caught me as I was walking out the door."

"A heavy date, Woody?"

"Don't be stupid! I'm on my way to catch a plane."

"I hope it isn't to Sacramento; they aren't expecting you. Mr. Brightbart says you haven't been there for two years."

There was the sound of heavy breathing on the other end. "Okay, so you know. What are you going to do about it?"

"My goodness, it doesn't matter to me," Pippa trilled. "Although Ray might take it hard, considering all those hefty expense accounts. Some of your friends in the front office might be a little disappointed in you too."

"Get to the point." Woody sounded like he was gritting his teeth. "What's your price?"

"Are you offering me a bribe?" Pippa was enjoying herself mightily.

"How much?" he gritted.

"I don't need money. We both make a good salary—although your fringe benefits are better than mine."

"How much?" he repeated heavily.

There was steel in Pippa's voice as she stopped playing games. "I ought to nail you for a bundle; that's the only thing that would really hurt. But I want something more important. From now on you're to leave Gloria strictly alone."

"Huh?" Woody couldn't believe she was serious.

"Get off Gloria's back," Pippa said succinctly. "If you ever harass her again, or threaten to tell her husband about that shabby incident, I'll crucify you. I'll not only tell Ray about your two-year free ride, I'll send a memo to everyone in the front office, and take out an ad in *Variety!*"

"What are you getting so worked up about?" he complained. "You'd think I was the only guy who ever padded an expense account."

"Padding is one thing, not even showing up is another," she replied curtly. "But that doesn't really interest me. It's what you did to Gloria that puts you beneath contempt." The disgust in her voice quivered over the wire.

"You don't have to be so goddamned holier than thou," he snarled. "What makes you think you're so great?"

"Walk softly, Woody," she warned. "If I weren't a better person than you, I'd turn in my membership card in the human race. Just remember what I said. One false move, and you're the has-been you ought to be."

Pippa was breathing hard when she slammed down the phone. It was too bad that she had to resort to blackmail, but someone like Woody only understood his own tactics. Besides, Gloria's need certainly outweighed the discomfort Pippa felt at sinking to Woody's level.

After she had composed herself, Pippa stopped by Gloria's desk. "Your fairy godmother finally got her act together. Woody won't be bothering you anymore."

Gloria turned startled eyes on her. "How do you know?"

"Just take my word for it," Pippa smiled.

Ordinarily Pippa enjoyed every moment of the working day, especially the newscast. It was satisfying to see her words come alive. This day was an exception. Knowing that Jeremy was waiting for her at the beach house drove Pippa wild. She thought the program would never end. To make matters worse, Ray chose this day to decide on a chat after air time.

He perched on the edge of her desk with the appearance of having all the time in the world. "That was a good story on the strike, Pippa. You certainly did your homework."

She knew this was Ray's way of apologizing for his

133

hesitation in sending her to Long Beach. Pippa acknowledged his thanks casually, not making too much of it.

"How's the investigation on Evergreen Elementary going?" he asked. "I think it's about time to do an update on that."

"As far as I know, there isn't anything new—at least nothing that they're releasing."

Ray gave her a penetrating look. "Were you just needling Woody when you said you had a pipeline to Jeremy Hawke?"

"I've been in contact with him," Pippa said carefully. "But he's pretty down on the media. It isn't easy to get anything out of him."

"How about a little human interest stuff? What he does for relaxation, for instance."

She glanced down at the desk, putting some papers into neat piles. "That's exactly the kind of thing he would hate. He's a very private man."

"A person in the public eye gives up that luxury." The speculation in Ray's eyes deepened. "You're too seasoned a reporter not to know that."

"I also have integrity," Pippa answered sharply. "I don't get my stories the way Woody does."

Ray continued to stare at her for a moment before sliding off the desk. "Well, keep after it." He grinned suddenly. "Now that the strike is settled, and the Dodgers are on the road, we need *something* to fill up the hour."

Pippa worried over the problem on the way to Malibu. The pressure was building on all sides. Maybe tonight she would be able to clear everything up with Jeremy. It would scarcely be auspicious to ask for a story at the same time, however. She sighed deeply, a vague uneasiness dimming her pleasure at seeing him again.

It didn't help matters that she was so much later than expected. Jeremy didn't reproach her, but he did ask if she minded skipping cocktails. They were having dinner at home and the housekeeper was waiting to serve.

Pippa felt guilty. "I'm sorry to have kept you, Mrs.

Dunphy. Why don't you run along? I'll do the cleaning up."

"That won't be necessary, Miss Alcott. It's what I'm paid for."

There was no hint of martyrdom in the woman's reply, just a flat statement of fact. She was working for the money, and would do whatever was necessary to earn it. That was certainly admirable, yet Pippa couldn't help being irritated. A little warmth would make her a lot easier to be around. Mrs. Dunphy was like a robot. Did she have any human emotions, any friendship or loyalty? Or was she programmed to function solely on the receipt of cash?

Pippa shrugged off her minor annoyance with the woman. The evening with Jeremy lay ahead.

His greeting had been satisfyingly ardent, but during dinner he seemed slightly distracted. At first Pippa put it down to constraint because of Mrs. Dunphy's presence. As dinner continued, she wasn't so sure. There were no lingering glances between them, no sense of urgency for the moment when they would be alone.

"Is anything wrong, Jeremy?" Pippa asked uncertainly.

"What could be wrong now that we're together?" The smile he gave her made Pippa's heart lurch.

It was an idyllic scene. Outside the picture window, dark surf boomed against the shore, sending up sprays of diamond in the moonlight. The wild elements lent a sense of coziness to the softly lit dining room where flickering candlelight imparted a feeling of intimacy.

"I just thought you seemed sort of far away."

"I'm sorry, darling." Jeremy's warm hand covered hers. "Maybe I was, but just for a minute."

"Is it anything you'd like to talk about?"

"You're the one I want to talk about," he said fondly. "How's school, honey?"

She lowered her lashes. "Just fine."

"How are you doing in accounting class? I'm beginning to be a little suspicious about that one." When her eyes flew open, Jeremy fixed her with a stern look. "I think it's just an excuse."

"Wha-what do you mean?"

He laughed. "Do you have something going with your professor? You were later than usual tonight."

Pippa's sense of relief was so strong that she felt dizzy for a moment. "If you need assurance, I'll be glad to provide it." Her voice was a little shaky.

Jeremy's eyes were smoky. "Don't think I won't take you up on that offer later."

When Mrs. Dunphy came in to clear the table, Pippa knew it was time to change the subject. "How is the investigation going, Jeremy? You haven't mentioned it for days."

"I haven't had my mind on it lately," he responded dryly.

Pippa knew he was referring to the recent upheaval in their relationship. A little smile played around her generous mouth as she acknowledged it. "Don't hand me that, Jeremy. You're like a bloodhound. I wouldn't want you on my case."

"Strange"—his dancing eyes belied the judicial tone of his voice—"I got the opposite impression."

Pippa wished Mrs. Dunphy would work a little faster. She was removing plates with maddening deliberation. Till she left the room, unstilted conversation was impossible.

"Really, Jeremy, what *is* going on?" Pippa asked, returning to the safe subject of the elementary school collapse. "By this time you must be seeing some daylight."

"We are," he responded grimly.

"From the look on your face I gather it wasn't an act of God."

He raised one eyebrow. "You can deduce that from a look?"

"You have a very expressive face." Pippa grinned impishly. "I'd like to play poker with you on a slow boat to China. At the end of the cruise you'd belong to me."

He gave her a melting smile. "I won't make the obvious answer."

Pippa forced down the rising tide of warmth that enveloped her. That would have to wait until later. "Come on, Jeremy, was it collusion, or was the contractor solely responsible?"

"You know I can't tell you that, Pippa," he said quietly.

The knowledge that he still didn't trust her was a bitter pill, flawing her happiness. "Why don't you tell it the way it is? You can, but you won't," she stated flatly.

His eyes were enigmatic. "If that's the way you want it."

"It isn't!" she cried. "But there's nothing I can do about it."

"Why does it mean so much to you?" he asked ominously.

"Because I want to share everything with you, not just —" Pippa stopped abruptly as Mrs. Dunphy brought in the coffee service.

"We'll have our coffee in the den," Jeremy instructed the housekeeper.

The den was a small room across the hall from the dining room. The person who had built the house evidently intended it as a place to work undistracted. Conventional windows looked out on the highway and the hills beyond instead of at the fascinating vista of the ocean.

They were both silent while the housekeeper put the tray on the coffee table. When she prepared to pour, Jeremy said, "We'll take care of that, Mrs. Dunphy." As soon as the woman had closed the door behind her, he turned to Pippa. "I thought we had this thing settled between us, but I see I was wrong."

"How can it be settled when you won't ever talk about it?" she cried passionately.

"You know how I feel about the necessity for secrecy. It's important that nothing leaks out to the public before the investigation is completed."

137

"Well, thanks a whole heap!" Pippa exclaimed indignantly. "It's nice to know I'm just part of the crowd."

Jeremy swore pungently. "That's too idiotic to refute."

"Your opinion of me grows more fascinating by the moment," she said icily.

He made a great effort to control himself. "Listen to me, Pippa. The way to keep a secret is not to tell *anybody.*"

"What do you think I'd do with the information?" she challenged him.

"Nothing!" He raked his fingers through his thick, dark hair. "Can't you understand that this has nothing to do with you?"

"I don't agree." Her eyes were steady on him. "The actual investigation might not, but your excluding me from it does."

"That's a contradiction," he objected.

"It's all part of the same thing. How do you think it makes me feel to know you don't trust me?"

"You can't possibly believe that," he denied vehemently. "I haven't held anything of myself back from you."

"Not your body," Pippa agreed sadly. "But you've never let me share any other part of your life. I get only tantalizing little glimpses."

The strain on his face was replaced by tenderness. "That's because we've had such a short time together, sweetheart." A light kindled in his eyes. "When we're together, conversation isn't uppermost in my mind."

"Mine either," she admitted honestly. "But I'd like to feel that I was more than just a warm body in your bed."

"Don't ever say that!" Jeremy took her hands, pulling her to her feet and into his arms. He buried his face in her hair, holding her in a tight embrace. "You have to know how much you mean to me."

It would have been so easy to relax against him and let the whole thing slide. His lithe, warm body was working its familiar magic on her, reminding her of the ecstasy it could convey. Pippa didn't even want the inside information for any reason. There was nothing she could honorably do with it.

She knew there was a very important principle involved though. It wasn't just pique that had prompted her challenge. She had to be an equal partner to Jeremy or it was no good. If all he wanted from her was sex, her days were numbered.

She forced herself to retreat from his arms. "The trouble is I *don't* know. There's no doubt that our physical relationship was put together by a celestial computer. Maybe that ought to be enough for me, but it isn't. That's why this investigation is so important. I want to share your confidences. I could tell immediately this evening that you were all keyed up about something. I want you to feel you can talk to me, get it all out of your system. If you can't do that, then I'm not very important to you. My function could be performed by almost any female."

Jeremy put his hands on her shoulders, staring at her as though seeing her for the first time. "I never realized I was doing this to you. Why didn't you tell me sooner?"

Pippa's smile was a little lopsided. "I guess I have to share the blame. As you said, there always seemed to be more urgent matters to take care of."

His hands tightened for a moment before he released her. "All I can do is ask forgiveness, my dear. I've been a loner all my life, and I guess old habits die hard. Please believe it wasn't because I didn't trust you." His hand caressed her cheek tenderly. "I would trust you with my life."

Pippa put her arms around his waist, smiling through a mist of tears. "That's only because you know how much it means to me."

Jeremy's embrace was convulsive, straining her against him so fiercely that Pippa felt bruised. She raised her face to his, parting her lips for his deeply satisfying kiss. But when her fingers lovingly traced his straining back muscles before slipping inside the waistband of his slacks, Jeremy captured her hands.

He kissed the tip of her nose, shaking his head at the

139

protest in her eyes. "Not yet, darling. We have a lot of things to straighten out."

It was what she wanted, yet when Pippa was this close to Jeremy, nothing seemed urgent except being in his arms. "You're right, but it can wait a little while," she murmured, twisting a button on his shirt so the curling hair was revealed in the widened V.

Once more he captured her hand, bringing it to his lips and kissing her fingertips. "Don't tempt me, honey." He pushed her gently down on the couch, seating himself in a leather chair a safe distance away. "I thought you knew how much you meant to me, Pippa. It hasn't all been making love. We've laughed together."

"But never talked," she said softly.

"Because I didn't want the world to intrude," he tried to explain. "Our time together is so precious. I wanted to keep you all to myself, to have you think only of me."

"Don't you see what that makes me, Jeremy? A wind-up doll programmed to make love when you push the right buttons. I have more to give you than that, and I want more from you. We don't even have to make love every time we see each other. If you're keyed up the way you were when I got here tonight, I'd be content just to sit and listen to your problems. I probably couldn't offer any constructive criticism, but just having a sounding board sometimes helps. When you constantly reject my efforts it makes me feel like a pampered pet—decorative, but not much else."

Jeremy got up to stand over her, lifting her chin in his hand. "I've really underestimated you, haven't I, Pippa?" He stared down at her exquisite features, a wealth of emotions coursing across his face. "You never told me how old you are, but it doesn't matter anymore, I see that now. You're all woman, my love," he told her softly.

Pippa stood up swiftly, moving into his arms. Her lips touched the strong column of his neck as she rested her head on his shoulder. "Oh, Jeremy, I'm so glad you finally found that out."

His hand caressed the length of her body, coming to

140

rest on the curve of her hip. "I regret the misunderstandings it caused, but I can't regret making love to you," he murmured huskily.

"I don't want you to," she breathed fervently, pulling his head down to hers.

As Jeremy's arms tightened, the telephone shrilled loudly. He groaned, resting his cheek against Pippa's soft hair before releasing her. "I'll get rid of whoever it is," he promised, his eyes smoldering down at her.

But after the first curt greeting, his annoyance vanished. It was Stretch on the phone, with news that affected Jeremy powerfully. He listened intently, interjecting a brief question every now and then, a frown of fierce concentration on his face.

Pippa realized from Jeremy's end of the conversation that something important had happened in the investigation. He had completely forgotten her presence. She could have stayed and listened, but the idea of eavesdropping on Jeremy now was repugnant. Pippa started quietly for the door.

"Don't go," Jeremy called to her surprise. As she turned back hesitantly, he waved her toward the couch. "That's it then!" he said exultantly into the phone. "We've got them cold." Jeremy hung up the receiver, his face a blaze of triumph.

"Is it all over?" Pippa asked uncertainly.

Her emotions were mixed. She was glad, of course, that the truth had been ferreted out, but couldn't it have waited a little longer? Tonight had been such a big step forward in her relationship with Jeremy. He had finally come to accept her as a woman in the fullest sense of the word. Given just a little more time, he might come to realize that he loved her. But if the investigation was over, Jeremy would return to Washington immediately. Did absence really make the heart grow fonder? Or would all his original doubts return once he was back in his own milieu? Would she become just a fond memory that would fade and merge with all the others he had? The idea was unbearable.

141

Jeremy was answering her question. "All over but the final wrap-up." His strong face expressed scorn. "Would you believe they were so cocky they didn't even destroy the evidence? We're going to move in before they know what hit them."

Pippa was intrigued in spite of her personal misery. "You say 'they.' Does that mean there's more than one person involved?"

Jeremy nodded. "We found out almost from the beginning that Carl Dabney, the contractor, used inferior material. What held us up for so long was getting proof that someone else was in on it with him."

Pippa's eyes were intent. "You almost had to know there was collusion. How else would he have gotten the building past inspection?"

"Knowing and proving are two different things."

"Did Dabney crack? Is that how you finally got the goods on them?"

Jeremy shook his head. "He doesn't know we have the evidence, neither of them does. That's why secrecy was so essential. We wanted to build an airtight case without depending on either one's rather dubious testimony." His mouth straightened to a grim line. "This is one net they're not going to slip out of. There's no excuse for that sort of greed."

"Who was the politician?" Pippa asked curiously. "Was it—"

Jeremy held up his hand suddenly. Gliding noiselessly to the door, he yanked it open. Mrs. Dunphy stood just outside, a surprised expression on her normally impassive face.

"I was just coming to tell you that I'm leaving now," the housekeeper said in her usual colorless voice, having regained her composure.

Jeremy's narrowed eyes surveyed her face, finding nothing there. "All right. Good night, Mrs. Dunphy. I'll see you tomorrow."

"You don't think she was listening, do you?" Pippa asked in concern.

"No, I guess it was just a coincidence." Jeremy jammed his hands into his pockets, scowling. "But now you see why caution has gotten to be almost a religion with me."

Pippa grew very still. "You're regretting the fact that you told me, aren't you?"

He stopped pacing, returning to clasp her slender shoulders in his big hands. "You know better than that." When she continued to look at him mutely, Jeremy chuckled. "I'll bet I can convince you."

Pippa sighed, lifting her face for his kiss. He would make love to her now and she would let him, because in spite of everything, she wanted him terribly. But nothing had really changed. The words Jeremy murmured into her ear brought Pippa's head snapping back.

"I'm going to tell you the name of the politician."

She looked at him searchingly. He really meant it! Fierce joy flooded Pippa as she flung her arms around his neck. "Oh, Jeremy, you don't have to do that! Just knowing you're willing to is enough."

He kissed the corner of her mouth tenderly. "I want to, sweetheart. There aren't ever going to be any secrets between us again. The man mixed up with—"

Pippa put her hand over his mouth. "Wait, don't say it. I think caution is catching." She went to the desk for a piece of paper, scribbling a name on it, then handing it to Jeremy. "Am I right?"

He smiled, nodding his head. "How did you get so smart?"

"I apply myself when I'm interested in the subject," Pippa grinned. She dropped the paper in a large ashtray, lighting it with a match.

Jeremy came up in back of her, linking his arms around her waist to pull her back against his hard body. He nuzzled her hair aside so he could kiss the sensitive spot at the nape of her neck. As the last scrap of paper curled into charred ashes, he murmured huskily, "If you're through tending that fire, I have another one you can put out."

They made love with the moonlight streaming over their bodies, turning Pippa's to creamy satin, and Jeremy's to golden bronze. His hands wandered tenderly over her, caressing, exploring, searching out the places he knew gave her the most pleasure.

Pippa explored his body, too, delighting in her ability to excite him. Her feathery caresses on his loins brought a sharp intake of breath as Jeremy wound his legs around hers, arching her body against his hard arousal. His mouth found her breast with sudden urgency, teasing given over to a need for fulfillment.

Pippa clasped her arms around his neck, her mouth meeting his with a hungry passion. They whispered endearments to each other, prolonging the ultimate moment until the exquisite agony had to be resolved. Responding to their mutual need, Jeremy staked the ultimate male claim, filling Pippa with such rapture that her body arched again and again in his arms, meeting his driving force with a like response.

The cresting wave tossed them higher and higher until they erupted in a calm sea that lapped gently around their relaxed bodies as it carried them gently back to shore. They remained clasped in each other's arms, joined in body and mind.

A little growl of satisfaction sounded deep in Jeremy's chest. "What did I ever do before I found you?"

That was something Pippa didn't want to think about. Nor what he planned to do after he left her. If only they had a little more time. She traced the plane of his high cheekbone. "You'll be leaving soon, won't you, Jeremy?"

He put his head on her breast, resting his lips on the silky skin. "That's something we have to talk about, but not tonight, sweetheart. Do you mind?" His eyelashes drooped and his head became heavier. "This day really took it out of me."

In just a few minutes Jeremy's even breathing told her he was asleep. She held him close, smoothing his dark hair and looking down at him tenderly.

Sleep didn't come to Pippa for a long time. All the

unresolved problems nagged at her, pulling her first one way and then another. What did Jeremy want to talk about? Was he framing a tactful good-bye, a considerate letdown? After the passion they had just shared it didn't seem possible, but she had been wrong before. Or was he going to say he couldn't live without her, that they would be married and live happily ever after? Pippa smiled ruefully at her own wishful thinking.

Well, the answer would have to wait until morning. And she'd better get some sleep in order to face it—whatever it was.

Pippa finally fell asleep, still clasped in Jeremy's arms.

CHAPTER NINE

Pippa wasn't destined to get her answer the next morning after all.

She awoke because Jeremy was staring at her with hungry intensity. As soon as her eyes opened he put his hand around the back of her neck, holding her for his lingering kiss.

"I didn't mean to wake you," he murmured, his green eyes glowing like a cat's. "I'm glad you're up though."

The heat of his body transferred itself to Pippa's. "Did you need me for something?" she asked mischievously, the mists of sleep abruptly dissipating.

Jeremy's hand closed over her breast, teasing the pink circle of satin into a coral pebble. "When didn't I?" his voice was throaty.

They had just stepped out of the shower when Rick Murphy phoned. Something urgent had come up that needed Jeremy's immediate attention.

"I hate to leave you like this." His mouth left hers reluctantly.

Pippa delicately licked a drop of water from his broad shoulder. "I think you effectively took care of everything," she murmured, laughing up at him through lowered eyelashes.

"You little vixen!" He tweaked the end of her tilted

146

nose. "You're being purposely seductive because you know I don't have time for a repeat performance."

"It's a subliminal suggestion." She pulled his towel free, and then her own. Instant electricity generated between them as their bare bodies met, fitting together like interlocking pieces of a puzzle. Pippa moved sensuously against him. "When you come home tonight, you'll be programmed to resume this position."

"As though I needed any urging," Jeremy scoffed, curving his hand under her buttocks to bring her closer to the juncture of his thighs. He groaned against her scented skin. "How am I ever going to talk to you when you keep distracting me like this?"

Pippa came back to earth abruptly. Jeremy was right; they had to talk. Was she purposely postponing it because she didn't want to hear what he had to say? That was cowardly, something she had never been. Pippa reached for their towels, handing one to him before wrapping hers around herself.

"All right, start talking. I promise to be good."

Jeremy pulled her towel down, bending his head to take one rosy nipple in his mouth. When he had finished his attentions it was stiff with excitement. "You're not only good, you're fantastic," he muttered. Pulling himself together with an effort, Jeremy reached for his shorts. "If I have time today, I'm going to pick up a chastity belt. Then maybe I'll be able to talk to you tonight."

Pippa didn't know if she could live through the day. "Is it important, Jeremy?"

He stroked her flushed, anxious face, a tenderness in his eyes that had nothing to do with desire. "The most important thing I've ever said to a woman," he murmured huskily.

"Tell me now," she pleaded.

"It's too earth-shattering to be rushed." He stared at her for a long moment, clearly shaken. With a little laugh he pulled on his slacks. "It will keep. Nothing is going to change between now and tonight."

Pippa was to remember that casual statement all the

days of her life, although at the time it was merely frustrating. Jeremy's whole attitude told her he was going to admit his love for her. Whether marriage was included didn't really matter right now. Her soft mouth curled in a smile as she faced the challenge. Once Jeremy let down his guard he was a goner. It was just aggravating to have to wait an entire day to hear the actual words.

Pippa didn't go into the newsroom that day. After Jeremy left she scurried around getting into her clothes, noting how scandalously late it was getting. A smile made her blue eyes sparkle like the sea outside as she recalled what had delayed them. She'd better phone, though, and tell Ray she was on her way.

"It's a good thing you called, Pippa. We just now got word that there's been an earthquake in Chatsworth." He named a small town in the environs of Los Angeles. "Pretty sharp one too. I want you to get up there on the double. The camera crew is already on its way."

"Got it, Ray." Pippa's agile mind was already figuring the fastest route.

"After you phone in the story, stick around there. Pick up some human interest stuff—how the roof caved in on the spot someone was standing in a minute before, or—hell, I don't have to tell you," he broke off, disgusted with himself.

"I know what you want," she assured him.

"I'll need the film and the camera crew back right away, but if you think it's necessary, you can keep one man."

When Pippa got to Chatsworth she found the devastation was fairly widespread, although fortunately no lives had been lost.

The next hours were hectic as she interviewed local officials and found out what safety measures were being taken. Pippa and the camera crew worked together with smooth professionalism amid the chaos, getting all the hard news.

After the crew went back to the city, Pippa switched to

the human interest angle, interviewing some of the survivors with tact and sympathy. Her ability to judge people and act accordingly was what made Pippa such an outstanding reporter.

It was a little after six by the time she got back to the newsroom, weary but exhilarated. The knowledge that she had done a good job, wringing out every drop of news without employing the obnoxious methods Woody used, was very satisfying. But her sense of well-being wasn't destined to last.

The newsroom was in a turmoil, with phones ringing and writers scurrying back and forth. This was a usual condition before air time, yet most peculiar once the program started.

"What on earth is going on?" Pippa asked Gloria.

"The miracle of the century—Woody pulled off a real coup." Gloria made a disgusted face. "There won't be any living with him after this one."

"What did he do?" Pippa stared at all the frantic activity, wondering what could have caused it.

"Don't ask me how, but he found out that Jeremy Hawke has the goods on Carl Dabney and some politician in that elementary school scandal."

"What!" Pippa clutched the edge of the desk to steady herself.

Gloria nodded as though it had been a question. "That's what all the fuss is about. The mayor and just about everyone else in City Hall have been demanding to know the politician's name. We've been fielding calls from the police too. They're not exactly ecstatic over a private investigator and a reporter finding out something that was right under their very own noses. They want to talk to Woody, but he's making himself scarce."

Pippa forced herself to appear calm. "This hasn't gone out over the air yet, has it?"

Gloria glanced at the wall clock. "It should be on about now. Your report on the earthquake was the lead story of course, but—" She stared after her friend's retreating figure.

Pippa dashed out the door and across the courtyard, bursting into the booth. Outside of the four men at the long counter in front of the bank of television screens, Woody was the only other person in the room. He was sprawled in a chair along the back wall, watching the proceedings.

His eyes gleamed with triumph as they rested on Pippa. "You're just in time, kiddo."

She ignored him, running down the aisle toward the producer, who turned to greet her. "Good story, Pippa," he nodded approvingly.

"Ray, I've got to talk to you," she jumped in breathlessly. "It's about the Evergreen investigation."

The producer glanced up at the screens. "It's coming on now."

With a sense of hopelessness Pippa watched the anchorman begin to read from the off-camera Tele-PrompTer.

"KCTV has just learned that there is definite proof of culpability in the collapse of the Evergreen Elementary School a few weeks ago. This channel's investigative reporter, Woody Phelan, was told that indictments are expected to be issued shortly against Contractor Carl Dabney and an unnamed politician. They will be charged with fraud and collusion in the substitution of inferior materials which were directly responsible for the devastating damages suffered by the school building."

There was more, but Pippa stopped listening. She felt as though someone had dealt her a mortal blow. How could Jeremy help but think she had been responsible for the leak? Even though Woody received credit for the story, Jeremy would think she had given it to him. And what would happen to all his work? Jeremy had stressed the need for secrecy in this final, crucial phase of the investigation. Would this allow Dabney and Maybeck to slip off the hook?

"Hey, Pippa," Woody called. "Who's got the last laugh now?"

She whirled around to face him. "How did you get that information?"

"Do you want to know how it's done?" he gloated.

"I *know* how it's done," she ground out furiously. "Like a pig roots for truffles!"

"You're just mad because all that pillow talk with the great stud didn't get you anywhere." Woody's eyes crawled over her like dirty fingers. "You should have used your head instead of your body."

Pippa's fingernails bit into her clenched palms. "What did *you* use, bribery?"

There was no doubt where Woody got his information. Mrs. Dunphy had been spying on them all through dinner. Pippa berated herself bitterly for not recognizing certain uncharacteristic actions—the way the housekeeper lingered over clearing the table, and the surprise on her face when Jeremy opened the door unexpectedly. Because Pippa had been too wrapped up in her own concerns to remember her training, Jeremy's work might be discredited.

"After you got your story didn't it ever occur to you to ask Hawke for confirmation?" she cried in frustration.

"That's like letting the farmer know you've stolen his chicken," Woody snorted.

"If you told him you already had the story, you could have bargained for an exclusive."

"I already have it," he informed her smugly.

"You fool!" she hissed. "Don't you realize by alerting those two men prematurely you probably blew the whole case? What's going to happen to your great fame as a reporter when no indictments are handed down?"

Uncertainty clouded his arrogant assurance. "Nobody could blame *me.*"

"I hope Dabney sues you for every penny of blood money you'll earn the rest of your life!" Pippa flung at him before racing out the door.

Back in the newsroom she pulled the telephone toward her without pausing to catch her breath. There was a chance that Jeremy hadn't listened to the six o'clock news. It was a slim chance, but the only one she had. If she could get to him first, maybe she could explain everything.

She let the phone ring endlessly at the beach house. Even if Jeremy wasn't home, Mrs. Dunphy ought to be there. Her blood boiled at the thought of talking to that female Judas, but it was vital to learn Jeremy's whereabouts. After fifteen rings Pippa was forced to give up. The housekeeper must have decamped, realizing the game was played out, Pippa reflected grimly.

Where else could Jeremy be? The possibilities were endless. Pippa was pulling out the phone directory when her question was answered.

Jeremy came storming into the newsroom, almost literally breathing fire. His eyes flashed with a blazing green light under peaked eyebrows that were drawn together in a ferocious scowl. Deep lines were grooved along his straight nose, leading to a mouth compressed in fury.

"I want to see an imbecile named Woody Phelan," he announced, sweeping the newsroom with a malevolent glare. His gaze swept past Pippa, and then snapped back. Surprise was quickly replaced by scorching contempt. "Well, well, all the vultures are in the same nest."

"Jeremy, I was trying to call you. It isn't the way you think," she began desperately.

"Pippa, will you have time to update the story on that chemical spill on the freeway?" a man across the room called. He put his hand over the mouthpiece of the phone on his shoulder. "I'm never going to get off the phone with Councilman Borg."

Jeremy's eyes narrowed suddenly. "I see what you mean. I've been had from all directions, haven't I?"

"Please, let me explain," she begged.

"There's no need. I came in in the middle of the picture, but I'm beginning to understand the plot." His smile was a ghastly travesty. "Local girl reporter puts one over on macho male; does whatever is necessary to get the story."

"No! It wasn't like that at all!"

"You put your whole heart and soul into the part, didn't you? No, let me amend that," he corrected himself. "I doubt whether you have either one."

"You've *got* to listen to me, Jeremy."

"I think you're in the wrong business," he continued inexorably. His lowered voice was nonetheless deadly. "The acting job you put on was worthy of an Oscar. Especially the part last night when you pretended you were more interested in making love than hearing the evidence." His eyes were bleak above the scornful twist of his mouth. "You really had me convinced. Doesn't that hand you a laugh?"

Pippa flinched, but she met his eyes steadily. "I didn't turn in that story."

"And you're not really a reporter," he remarked sardonically. "Just a little college girl who got lost on her way to accounting class."

"I don't deny that I'm a reporter, or that I should have told you long ago," she said quietly. "I know you won't believe this, but I wanted to tell you almost from the very beginning." She looked down at the desk. "Only I was afraid."

"Afraid you wouldn't get the story," he agreed disgustedly.

Pippa's eyes were sad as she gazed at the man she loved and knew she could never have now. "I was afraid if I told you the truth I wouldn't see you anymore."

The hard contempt on his face softened slightly as he looked at her searchingly. Various emotions struggled for supremacy—disbelief, uncertainty, and a dawning hope. "God, how I wish I could believe you, Pippa!"

"That's the honest truth, I swear it," she answered simply. "I couldn't betray you, Jeremy."

Woody stood in the doorway, surveying them maliciously. As Jeremy moved a step closer to Pippa, he sauntered over. "Is this guy trying to intimidate you, babe?" Turning to Jeremy, he said, "No reason to get steamed. She was just doing her job."

"You're lying!" Pippa cried. "If I had turned in that story, why would I let you take credit for it?"

Woody looked uncomfortable. "Gee, did I speak out of turn? I'm sorry if I blew it, Pippa. I didn't mean to queer your chances for getting more information."

As Pippa gazed at him in revulsion, Jeremy stared grimly down at the shorter man. "I gather you're Woody Phelan, Mata Hari's alter ego."

"Isn't she something else?" Woody commented admiringly. "When we made that bet I didn't think she had a prayer of pulling it off, but damned if she didn't do it."

"What bet?" Jeremy asked ominously.

"The bet we had that she could get the story out of you. Here's your payoff, Pippa." Woody drew out his money clip, peeling off some bills. "I have to admit you won it fair and square."

She pushed the money away violently. "It isn't true, Jeremy! I mean we did have a bet, but it was only that I could get an interview. I meant it when I said I would never use anything you told me off the record."

She might have been talking to herself. At the terrible look in Jeremy's eyes something shriveled up and died inside Pippa. After a choking moment of silence he reached into his pocket. Clenching a handful of coins, he threw them on the desk.

"I don't know if there are thirty pieces of silver there, but I hope it's enough to satisfy you." Jeremy turned and walked out the door.

Pippa could only watch him go, her heart shattering in a million pieces.

"I guess that makes us even." Woody's gloating voice was like a rasp on her battered nerves.

"You bastard," she said in a low, deadly voice.

"Sticks and stones," he replied mockingly.

"I didn't know anyone could sink as low as you. You got your story, wasn't that enough? Why did you have to credit it to me?"

"You gave me the idea in the booth just now." Woody's

raillery disappeared. "If there are any repercussions, I'm not taking the rap alone."

She regarded him impassively. "I think this time you've painted yourself into a corner. You took on screen credit for this little fiasco. There's no way you can shift the blame now."

As it happened, she underestimated Woody.

Pippa was so heartsick that all she wanted to do was get away by herself. She was like a small wounded animal. Last night her life had been bright with promise. Jeremy had been on the verge of making a commitment, she was sure of that. They could have had a lifetime of happiness together. How could it all have been swept away by one subhuman man with a grudge against her?

Pippa let herself into her apartment, feeling a hundred years old. If only there were some way to salvage the situation, but she knew there wasn't. Woody had spoken just enough of the truth to make her position untenable. She had admitted to the bet because she didn't want there to be any more lies between Jeremy and herself. It wouldn't have made any difference though. All the evidence was against her. Woody had seen to that. It might have cheered Pippa to know that he wasn't having an easy time of it.

Pippa hadn't been gone more than ten minutes before the police arrived in the newsroom. The importance of the mission was underlined by the fact that it was headed by Captain Fogarty, a gray-haired, cheerless man. To provide further emphasis, he was accompanied by two aides, Lieutenant Cresswell and Sergeant Green, both large, beefy, taciturn men. They headed for Woody, shepherding him into Ray's office.

Woody started out on the offensive. "I don't have to tell you guys anything. Haven't you ever heard of freedom of the press?"

Captain Fogarty regarded him with ill-concealed loathing. "That doesn't give you any right to break the law."

"Who said I did?" Woody asked belligerently.

The policeman had gotten himself under control.

"That's what we're here to find out. How did you discover there was negligence involved in the construction of Evergreen Elementary?"

"That's privileged information," Woody returned confidently.

"I'm not asking who your source was," the captain probed. "I only want to know if you're sure of your facts."

"Take my word for it," Woody advised smugly.

"Why should I if you won't give me any names? It could all be pie in the sky."

"Let's just say I got it from that old faithful—an unimpeachable source." Woody was starting to enjoy himself.

Fogarty settled his huge bulk in the chair. He had five hours until he went off duty. "We're not talking about some minor hood here. You've impugned the reputation of a reliable contractor and a politician."

"I notice you didn't attribute that noble quality to the politician," Woody needled.

Fogarty blinked, his only sign of emotion. "What's his name?"

Woody feigned ignorance. "Who?"

"If you have evidence linking someone in government to this incident, it's your duty to come forward with the information." The captain sounded like he was reading someone his rights.

"Why ask me? If you guys flubbed the ball, it isn't my concern," Woody remarked airily. "Some of us do our jobs better than others."

Despite his stoic exterior, Captain Fogarty had limits —and he had just reached them. "Listen to me, you two-bit pencil-pusher," he snarled. "There's nothing I'd like better than nailing your putrid hide to the masthead. If you don't level with us, I'm going to get you for everything from double-parking to spitting on the sidewalk!"

Woody was shaken by the change in the big man, although he tried to hide it with bluster. "That's intimidation. You might get away with it with the citizenry, but I'm part of the media."

"See how far that gets you when I haul you up in front of the judge for obstruction of justice."

"I don't have to disclose my sources," Woody insisted.

"And I don't have to handcuff you unless I feel you might try to escape." The captain nodded to his lieutenant, who reached for the cuffs at his belt. "I'm sure your station will bail you out, but I don't think you're going to enjoy your stay in the tank."

Woody's furious thoughts were visible in his furtive eyes. "There's no need to overreact, Fogarty. I didn't say I wouldn't cooperate."

"You media types think it's a big joke to make the police look like clowns. Well, I'd like to know who the public calls on when they're in trouble, their local television station?" Fogarty's jaw was set grimly.

Woody attempted to placate him. "Look, we all appreciate the cops. This whole thing is getting blown out of proportion. It's just another case of somebody getting caught with his hand in the cookie jar. It happens all the time."

The captain's steely eyes riveted him. "What's the politician's name?"

"I don't know it," Woody answered hopelessly.

Fogarty nodded to his aide. "Cresswell . . ."

"No, wait! I'm giving it to you straight. This wasn't really my story. It was Pippa Alcott's."

"We heard you got credit over the air."

"That's only because she couldn't take credit for it herself," Woody offered eagerly.

The captain's expression of contempt deepened. "If you're going to hide behind someone, couldn't you at least make it a man?"

"You don't understand," Woody began desperately. "It was Pippa's story all along. She was the one who was doing all the legwork to get the information from Hawke."

"And after she got it she passed it on to you out of the goodness of her heart," Fogarty remarked ironically.

"No, she . . . well, she didn't want Hawke to know

she was the source. Look, I'll level with you. Pippa is having an affair with Hawke. Everything she learns from him, she passes on to me."

Fogarty's features contorted in an expression of disgust. "And to think I ever thought the vice squad was slimy!"

"I'm not looking for Brownie points; I'm telling you the truth." Woody shot a sly look at the captain's face.

"Okay, so she's sleeping with the guy," Fogarty said heavily. "So who's the politician?"

"That's just it, he didn't tell her yet." Woody's leer was meant to include them both as men of the world. "He doled out payment for services received, and she hadn't gotten to that point yet."

Fogarty's stolid regard was expressionless. "If you're lying to me, Phelan, I'm going to find a reason to put you away."

"Why would I lie?" Woody tried to appear the picture of innocence, failing abysmally.

"To save your worthless skin, for one thing," Fogarty answered contemptuously. "You and this Alcott dame are a rare pair."

"I wasn't aware that this was a popularity contest," Woody said sharply.

"Lucky for you." A pregnant silence fell as the captain stared at him thoughtfully. A fine dew of perspiration broke out on Woody's forehead in spite of his efforts to appear unconcerned. Finally Fogarty asked, "Are you willing to swear you don't know who the politician is?"

"Of course! I'll even sign a paper if you like."

"Are you also willing to swear that Miss Alcott doesn't know either?"

Woody's eyes shifted. "You can't ask me to answer for somebody else."

"I can't ask you what time it is and expect a straight answer."

"You guys are really something else!" Woody's natural belligerence reasserted itself. "You expect the rest of us to do your job for you. I don't know if Pippa has the information you're looking for. Why the hell don't you go and ask her instead of sitting on your cans around here and harassing me?"

Fogarty got to his feet, his men following suit. "That's the only helpful suggestion you've made all evening, Mr. Phelan. I'm going to do just that. But don't think you're off the hook. I'll be talking to you again."

"It will be a pleasure, Captain," Woody answered mockingly, relieved now that the pressure was off.

Fogarty paused on his measured way to the door. "Don't count on it. I'll make sure you don't enjoy yourself."

He made a detour around Ray, who looked after the three big men with a puzzled frown. "Who were they?" he asked Woody.

"Can't you recognize the fuzz when you see them?" Woody's relief made him almost euphoric. "Those feet could fill the footprints of the abominable snowman."

"The police?" Ray asked sharply. "What are they doing here? Why didn't you call me?"

"No sweat. It was just routine harassment."

"What's going on, Woody?" Ray frowned.

"Pippa got herself in a bind," Woody remarked negligently.

"What are you talking about?"

"It's that Jeremy Hawke story. The cops want to know where she got her information."

Ray gave him a piercing look. "I thought that was your story."

"Oh, well, sure, but Pippa was helping me."

"The only way Pippa would ever help you is by kicking out the chair if you had a rope around your neck," Ray said succinctly. "Now get the hell out of my office while I find out what this is all about!"

CHAPTER TEN

Pippa considered ignoring the doorbell when it rang even as she realized the futility of such an act. Ray had alerted her that the police would be paying a visit. It wasn't likely they'd give up merely because she failed to answer the door.

With a deep sigh she levered her slender figure out of the armchair, facing the ordeal ahead with indifference. Pippa was dimly aware that there was great pain under her present lethargy, but she pushed the knowledge from her consciousness. Nothing could hurt her as long as she continued to exist in this vacuum.

"Miss Alcott? We have some questions we'd like to ask you," Captain Fogarty stated formally.

Pippa silently gestured the three men inside. When they were seated in her small living room Fogarty began the interrogation, making no pretense that it was anything else.

"I won't waste time, Miss Alcott," he said grimly. "Woody Phelan indicated that you know the name of the politician under investigation by Jeremy Hawke. We want that name."

"Surely you're aware that I'm not required to divulge the source of my information, Captain," Pippa returned steadily.

"I'm not asking your source; we already know that."

His eyes went over her slender body with distaste. "I want that name."

She shook her head. "I can't tell you. It would jeopardize a great deal at this point."

The big man gritted his teeth. "This isn't a court of law. You can't invoke the fifth amendment."

He thought she was trying to protect herself. As if it mattered, Pippa reflected wearily. "I can't tell you what you want to know."

"Do you deny having the information?" Fogarty demanded.

"No, I don't deny it." What was the point?

His inability to shake her unnatural calm was having the opposite effect on the captain. His face reddened angrily. "This isn't a game we're playing, Miss Alcott. You're either going to give me that information or you'll have a long time to think it over in jail."

She raised her eyebrows. "On what charge?"

"Obstructing justice, failing to cooperate with an officer, deliberate deception—you name it. We'll find something that will stick."

The questioning went on for a long time, with the other two men joining in. They took turns trying to wear her down, becoming more frustrated at the lack of effect it was having.

For Pippa it was just something to be gotten through, although she wished they would go away and leave her alone. Her head was beginning to ache from their loud voices. Couldn't they see they were wasting their time? She would never betray anyone's confidence, least of all Jeremy's. It was the one last thing she could do for him.

They finally left with ominous warnings, so it didn't surprise Pippa when two uniformed policemen showed up in the newsroom the next day.

One of them looked with interest around the big room while the other addressed Pippa formally. "We have a summons for you to appear before Judge Blackburn. Will you come with us now, Miss Alcott?"

Someone had alerted Ray, who came surging out of his

office. "What's going on?" he asked. After the officer had repeated his request, Ray demanded, "What are the charges?"

"There aren't any charges yet. Judge Blackburn merely wishes to speak to Miss Alcott in his chambers."

"Oh, no! Anything he has to say to her is going to be said in open court," Ray declared. "I'm coming with you, Pippa. Gloria, get our lawyers on the phone. Have them meet us downtown." His orders were barked out crisply.

Judge Blackburn was less than pleased at the crowd that surrounded Pippa. News of her possible arrest had spread swiftly through the indefinable grapevine used by the media. Besides Ray and her attorneys, there were reporters from the various newspapers, radio, and television stations. As furious as the judge was about it, he was forced to hold an open hearing.

Ray's indignation had been mounting ever since the policemen appeared in the newsroom. As the judge frowned at Pippa, it boiled over. He jumped to his feet. "Your honor, I have something to say. Pippa Alcott is an accredited, conscientious reporter. You have no right to drag her down here like a common criminal. I say charge her with something or let her go!"

Judge Blackburn's frown deepened. "If *you* don't want to be charged with contempt of court, you'll sit down and be quiet."

A flicker of amusement penetrated Pippa's depression. She tugged at Ray's arm. "Get off my case, will you, Ray?" she whispered. "If you don't stop helping, they're going to charge me with treason at the very least." Her smile vanished as the duel of wits began.

The judge started out impassively. "I'm told you have in your possession the name of the politician under suspicion in the Evergreen affair."

Pippa nodded. "That's correct, your honor."

"I'm ordering you now to divulge that name."

Her back was very straight. "It isn't mine to give."

"Correction, young woman. You have no right to keep

162

it to yourself," the judge said sternly. "Don't you realize you could be abetting a criminal?"

"That's exactly why I can't tell you, your honor. The . . . the person who told me the man's name stressed the need for secrecy so the guilty parties wouldn't be alerted. He was afraid they would try to cover up."

"Unless they're both blind and deaf, they must have some inkling by now that they're being investigated," the judge said sarcastically. "Your own station broke the story on the news last night."

It was what had haunted Pippa ever since. But it still wasn't up to her to reveal the information. Besides her obligation to Jeremy, there was a principle involved. Judge Blackburn didn't see it that way. He became increasingly testy as she remained adamant. It didn't help matters that the crowd was completely partisan. When they became too exuberant he rapped his gavel repeatedly, threatening to throw one or another of the reporters out of the courtroom.

After it became obvious that Pippa wasn't going to capitulate, Judge Blackburn's manner hardened. "In the face of your flagrant defiance of the law, Miss Alcott, you leave me no choice," he said grimly. "I'm going to be forced to send you to jail."

Bedlam broke out in the courtroom, with everyone talking at once. Even Pippa's attorneys couldn't make themselves heard.

When order was finally restored, the judge stared down at her. "I'll give you exactly forty-eight hours to change your mind. At the end of that time, you'll be sent to the county jail, where you will remain until you furnish us with the information in your possession."

Pippa felt rather dazed as she was whisked out of the courtroom, surrounded by well-wishers. The possibility of this had occurred to her, of course, but she hadn't seriously considered it. What would jail be like? Because that's where she was going. She had no choice. Pippa felt a slight shiver travel down her spine at the idea of being locked in a barred cell.

"Keep your chin up, Pippa," one of the rival reporters advised. "We're with you all the way."

"That's right. You're doing it for all of us," another man declared.

Back in Ray's office they had a meeting with the lawyers, who admitted there wasn't much they could do. Ray was taking it worse than Pippa. After the attorneys left, he flung himself in his chair, raking his fingers through his hair.

"Damn it, Pippa, I wish there were some way out of this mess!"

"This too shall pass," she commented, striving for a light tone.

"It's not going to be any picnic," he said sharply. "Once all the hoopla dies down, you're going to be in there with God knows what kind of people."

"I know," she answered quietly.

"I don't like it," Ray declared, getting to his feet to pace the floor.

Pippa gave him the ghost of a smile. "It isn't exactly my first choice either."

He stopped pacing to stare down at her, brooding. "I would never admit it to that judge, but one thing he said did make sense. The culprits in the case have already been put on their guard."

Her eyes held his steadily. "Are you asking me to violate the basic principles of journalism?"

"You know I wouldn't do that, Pippa. I'm just suggesting that maybe you're offering yourself as a sacrificial lamb when the rites are already over."

"I don't mean to sound dramatic, but the freedom of the press is involved here, Ray. If we can be intimidated by *anyone,* then it's just a small step to being influenced."

He nodded in resignation. "You're right of course."

"I wish I didn't have to go to jail to prove such an obvious point, but I don't see what else I can do."

Ray's eyes gleamed with sudden hope. "I just had a thought! Since there's no question that the politician—whoever he is—and I'm not asking his name," he added hastily. "Anyway, he's already been alerted, so maybe Hawke will come forward with his name."

Pippa's long lashes dropped. "Not a chance."

Ray was charged with new enthusiasm. "You don't know that. Okay, so he's pretty sore about the story being leaked, but you didn't do it, Woody did. Why would Hawke take it out on you?"

"He isn't too fond of any of the media," she said hopelessly.

"Even so, he wouldn't be *that* vindictive!"

"Just take my word for it. Jeremy Hawke wouldn't lift a finger to help me."

Ray fell silent, obviously searching for a tactful way to express himself. "Look, Pippa, I heard the story Woody told the police. I figured it was all garbage, a cornered rat trying to lay off the blame. But if there's a grain of truth to it, that's all the more reason why you've got to get in touch with Hawke."

"I can't," she said in a low, tortured voice.

"Then I will."

"No! Leave it alone, Ray!" When he looked at her doubtfully, Pippa attempted to smile. "You know what happens to well-intentioned third parties."

"I'm not trying to intervene in a lovers' quarrel. You can make that up between yourselves later," Ray said impatiently.

If he had seen the look of contempt on Jeremy's face as he left the newsroom, Ray would realize the futility of that statement. Pippa could only hope time would erode the terrible memory. That some day she'd be able to remember Jeremy as the tender lover he had once been—and would never be again.

A deep sigh shuddered through her as she faced the bleak prospect. It was her own private hell, though, not something anyone could help her with. Pippa tried to shrug off her deep depression.

"I appreciate your concern, Ray, but if you really want to do something constructive, you can bake me a cake with a file in it."

After a heavy moment of silence he tried to match her light tone. "You've got it, Ace." Ray's smile didn't reach his eyes.

Pippa got to her feet, squaring her slim shoulders. "Well, I'd better get to work. I'm not on vacation at the government's expense yet."

"Why don't you take the day off, Pippa?"

"And do what, smell the flowers? Cheer up, Ray, this won't be my last chance. They parole even murderers these days," she teased, touched by his woebegone expression.

"I just thought maybe you had some things to do before—"

"I'll have all day tomorrow for that. Let's see . . . forty-eight hours will put it at about eleven in the morning, day after tomorrow."

Pippa tried to concentrate on finishing stories she had been drafting, turning over to other writers those that were pending. She was interrupted constantly by calls from friends and colleagues. Although she appreciated the outpouring of affection, she would have preferred to lose herself in work. Trying not to hurt anyone's feelings, she turned down all invitations, knowing that no amount of company could fill the awful emptiness inside her.

The morning newspapers announced her impending incarceration on the front page. The general public, after hearing the story on every newscast, might have considered it much ado about nothing, but to the media it became a cause célèbre. One of their own was being threatened. Unfortunately, the impassioned prose and editorializing produced a no-win situation. After all the glare of publicity, Judge Blackburn couldn't have backed down even if he'd wanted to.

Pippa insisted on working straight through the newscast, treating it like any other day. She was relieved that in the rush of getting the program on the air, everyone finally forgot about her. All except Woody. He had made himself extremely scarce during the frenetic uproar, but he finally forced himself to approach Pippa when he found her alone in the newsroom.

"I guess I owe you an apology," Woody said with a diffidence she had never seen before. "I never thought this thing would blow up into such a donnybrook."

Pippa regarded him calmly. "I suppose I should be saintly and tell you it's all right—but I'm not going to. The only good thing about going to jail is the vacation I'll get from you."

Woody's eyes flickered away from hers. "If there's anything I could do . . ."

"Self-immolation might help for starters, but I guess you're not that good a sport." Pippa swept him with a disdainful glance before getting up and walking out of the room.

At the end of the show Pippa once more had to fend off invitations.

"I wish you'd reconsider about staying over with Scott and me," Gloria continued to implore. "You shouldn't be alone tonight."

"I have a million things to do," Pippa assured her. "I'm going to wash my hair and do my nails to begin with." She smiled at their worried faces. "You wouldn't want me to disgrace the station in front of all those cameras."

"At least have dinner with me," Ray urged. "I promise not to talk about it. We'll just have a few laughs."

When it was apparent that Pippa really meant her refusals Gloria said, "Well, if you should change your mind and get lonesome or . . . or anything, just give me a call. I can be at your place in ten minutes."

"I promise. Now, will all of you let me get on with my self-beautification program?" Pippa joked.

It was a relief to get home, away from all the well-meant solicitude. Pippa unlocked her door, stopping in her tracks to stare in disbelief. Directly facing her was a huge horseshoe entirely covered with roses. A satin banner across it held the legend GOOD LUCK. It was the kind of adornment placed over a winning horse. Pippa's laughter was completely genuine as she reached for the card wired to the side. It was from her friends at the press club.

Her attention was drawn to other bouquets scattered around the room, and Pippa's eyes misted over. Such good friends. At least she had done one thing right in her life.

"I'm so glad you're home, Miss Alcott." Pippa's landlady had been lying in wait for her. "I've been worrying the whole afternoon about letting those people into your apartment, but I didn't know what else to do with all those flowers."

"It's okay, Mrs. Dalrymple," Pippa smiled.

"They're just gorgeous, aren't they? My goodness, I don't know when I've ever seen such a display."

Except at a funeral, Pippa reflected dryly. Or a wedding? Her mind shivered away from that thought. "Yes, they are lovely."

The landlady voiced Pippa's earlier conclusion. "You certainly have a lot of friends."

Pippa's smile became rather fixed. "I'll have to remember that and count my blessings."

The older woman drew the wrong conclusions. "I heard about your . . . uh . . . your trouble. I want you to know how sorry I am." Indignation overcame embarrassment. "It's a crying shame, that's what it is! Why aren't the police out catching criminals instead of putting an honest, hard-working woman like you in prison?"

"I'm not exactly going to prison," Pippa said gently. "Just the county jail."

"That's bad enough. It's certainly no place for a decent young girl. My blood runs cold when I think what can happen to you in a place like that!"

The landlady's well-intentioned sympathy wasn't very comforting. While Pippa looked for a way to escape it, her eyes lit on the floral offerings. "You do volunteer work at Children's Hospital, don't you, Mrs. Dalrymple?

How would you like to take all these flowers down there?"

"Oh, that would be just grand! The children would be so thrilled, and the nurses would too."

"Good. Then why don't you make arrangements to have the whole lot picked up?"

"Are you sure? Your friends sent them to you."

"I appreciate their thoughtfulness, and I'll enjoy the flowers even more knowing they're not going to waste. Will you excuse me, that's my phone."

It was only the first of many calls. Finally Pippa took the telephone off the hook. The only person she wanted to talk to wasn't going to call.

Pippa did both of the things she said she was going to do. After washing her hair she blew it dry, brushing it into a sun-kissed, pale brown cloud around her slim shoulders. The polish she chose for her nails was a bright, defiant red. After packing a few things in a bag, there really wasn't anything else to do.

She turned on the television, but it failed to hold her interest. Then she tried to read, with the same result. Finally Pippa gave up and let her thoughts drift to Jeremy. Was he pleased that retribution had overtaken her? Was he deriving grim satisfaction from the knowledge that she was being punished for her sins? If he only knew how much!

With a deep sigh she reached into the dresser for a clean nightgown, becoming very still when she saw which one she had chosen. It was the yellow chiffon.

After a long moment Pippa drew it out of the drawer. It was only the first of the myriad things that would remind her of Jeremy. There was no point in trying to avoid it. She might as well face facts and learn to live with them.

But when Pippa pulled the fragile garment over her head, she started to tremble. The memories it brought back were unbearable. She could almost feel Jeremy's hands shiveringly seductive as they explored her body through the thin veil of silk. She remembered how the slow caresses had built in tempo until they were both on fire, needing each other as never before. Their union had been all the more intense because of their brief estrangement. Jeremy had lifted her from the depths of despair to the height of ecstasy by resolving all the misunderstanding between them.

Pippa threw herself across the bed, the tears she had held back suddenly coming in a torrent. "Oh, Jeremy, I let you explain. Why wouldn't you listen to *me?*"

In a hotel room not far away, the eleven o'clock news was rolling the final credits. Rick Murphy snapped it off. "Well, tomorrow is Pippa's big day."

"I hate to see her go to jail," Stretch answered slowly.

"Do you know of anyone who deserves it more?"

"Oh, come on, that's pretty extreme," Stretch protested.

"Not in my book!" Rick scowled. "She could have endangered the whole operation."

"She wasn't the one who leaked the story. It was that guy—Woody something-or-other."

"After she passed on the information. They were in it together. You don't honestly think it's just a coincidence that they both worked for the same TV station?"

"I guess not," Stretch admitted reluctantly. "But if that's so, why did they hold Maybeck's name back? Why is Pippa going to jail over it?"

"A grandstand play to get more publicity," Rick answered disdainfully. "She won't go through with it. Wait till all the cameras are rolling tomorrow. She's going to have a sudden change of heart."

"I don't think so," Stretch remarked thoughtfully. "Pippa didn't strike me as a phony that night we were all together."

"I'd like to know your definition of one then," Rick exploded. "That wide-eyed college girl routine, and pretending all she wanted to know was what the great man had for breakfast."

"That was a bummer," Stretch admitted.

"You bet your pension! No wonder Jeremy is too embarrassed to face anyone. It isn't like him to be taken in that way."

"We were too," Stretch reminded him.

"But we didn't tell her anything," Rick pointed out. "I wonder how the hell she wormed the information out of him."

Stretch raised mocking eyebrows. "That's a pretty stupid question."

"Jeremy's a pro when it comes to women," Rick protested. "I can see him sleeping with her, but I can't imagine him getting that carried away."

"Pippa's a lot of woman," Stretch reflected. He grinned suddenly. "I know *I'd* have told her anything she wanted to know."

"But not Jeremy," Rick insisted. "It isn't like he's a kid, all excited about a roll in the hay."

"Maybe she's more to him than that." Stretch looked thoughtful. "Remember that night at his place? When I suggested riding home with Pippa, Jeremy cut me out very neatly."

"Only because he decided to give her the interview she wanted."

"Why the sudden change of heart after he'd refused all evening? No, I think he was putting the off-limits sign on Pippa, and a man doesn't do that to a woman he feels casual toward."

"If you're right, it makes her even worse. She deliberately set the guy up for the Judas kiss."

"You don't know that. In fact, the evidence is all to the contrary. She's going to jail rather than reveal the information Jeremy gave her."

Rick smiled sardonically. "I never knew you were such a romantic. Pippa loves Jeremy, and Jeremy loves Pippa, right? So how come he took off for San Francisco and left us here to finish up?"

Stretch shrugged. "He's been working hard and it's all over but the formalities. We've got both of those guys cold."

"I'll pass over the fact that he'd take her with him—especially if relaxation was what he had in mind. Just tell me why he's letting his lady love go to jail if he thinks she's as innocent as you do."

Stretch looked unhappy. "That's the thing that's worrying me."

"It isn't worrying Jeremy," Rick stated with satisfaction. "He's getting his revenge and loving it."

Stretch shook his head. "That's out of character. He might blister her with every word in the English language, but he wouldn't allow anything to happen to her. There's an old-fashioned streak of chivalry in Jeremy that wouldn't let any woman get hurt—especially one he once loved."

"He's doing it."

"Maybe he doesn't know what's been happening." Stretch's brow furrowed. "That ranch he told us about is out in the country somewhere."

"I have a flash for you," Rick said mockingly. "Even in the country they have that wonderful new invention called television, not to mention newspapers and radio."

"This is a local thing," Stretch persisted. "They wouldn't make as big a deal out of it up north."

"I imagine they'd give it a passing mention," Rick answered dryly. "It *is* a news story, no matter how minor."

Stretch got to his feet, jamming his hands into his pockets. "I think we ought to call him anyway, just in case."

"And say what? I hear your girlfriend's off to the lock-up tomorrow. Do you want us to send your regards?" Rick made a face. "He'd bite our heads off. Jeremy's not a guy who likes his privacy invaded."

"I know that. I just think there's been some kind of a misunderstanding," Stretch insisted doggedly.

"Well, I'm not about to get in the middle of it. And if you're smart, you won't either. Come on, let's turn in."

172

"I guess you're right." Stretch started to follow Rick, halting after a few steps. "Hell, I'm never going to be able to sleep. You're probably right on target and I'll get my head handed to me, but I've got to call Jeremy."

CHAPTER ELEVEN

The lovely countryside surrounding Jeremy's ranch wasn't affording him the pleasure it usually did.

After storming out of the newsroom he had gotten into his car and headed north instinctively. He had taken the longer coastal route, needing the challenge of twisting mountain roads rather than the monotony of the straight freeway.

The beautiful scenery might not have existed. The foaming breakers crashing on deserted shores at the bottom of steep cliffs were ignored as he took the curves at tire-protesting speed, proving his mastery over the powerful car.

He had arrived at the ranch in the middle of the night, tired enough to sleep. But at daybreak Jeremy was awake. After a quick shower he donned jeans and a plaid shirt before going down to the stable where his favorite stallion, Midnight, welcomed him with a soft nicker of joy.

Diaphanous mist cloaked the mountaintops as Jeremy rode through the silent, diamond-dewed meadows. He threw his head back, inhaling the crisp, clean air and waiting for the exultation that didn't come.

By the time he returned to the house an hour later, he was in a foul mood. Had she even spoiled this for him?

174

Mary O'Malley, his housekeeper, greeted him with astonishment. "What are you doing here?"

"I live here." Jeremy's reply was uncharacteristically curt.

She was silent for a long moment, assessing the climate. Jeremy was usually not only unfailingly polite, he was more like a friend than an employer. Mary and her husband, Mike, had worked on the place as caretakers for almost ten years. In that time they had watched Jeremy's business grow from a fledgling enterprise into a giant corporation. They had also kept an eye on his active private life. Mary took an almost maternal interest, although she was only seven years older than Jeremy. She worried now about what could be bothering him.

"If you'd told us you were coming, I would have had your room aired out," she said tentatively.

"I wouldn't have noticed." Realizing that he was being churlish, he gave her a strained smile. "I was so tired when I got in that I could have slept on the floor."

"Where did you come from?" she asked curiously.

"Los Angeles. I drove." His tone discouraged comments.

"Are you home to stay now?"

"No, I'll have to go back to L.A. in a couple of days." His eyes were bleak.

Mary looked at him in concern. "You look so tired."

He sighed. "I am. Bone weary."

"Why don't you stop all this nonsense and come home where you belong?" she cried, wanting to comfort him without knowing what for.

"Maybe I will at that." His shoulders had a discouraged slump. "I need to come back to my own world," he muttered. "At least computer readouts don't lie."

"I'll bet you haven't had any breakfast," Mary said abruptly. Food was her answer to most of life's problems, as evidenced by her full figure. "Come in the kitchen and I'll make you some bacon and eggs."

"Thanks, but I'm not hungry." Jeremy disappeared down the hall.

She watched him go, shaking her head. In the kitchen a short time later Mary discussed it with her husband.

"I've never seen him like this before. What on earth do you think could be wrong? It couldn't be business worries. Hawke Electronics is like a license to print money."

"Sounds like woman trouble to me," Mike remarked, unfolding his napkin.

"Don't be ridiculous! Jeremy needs a fly swatter to keep them away."

"There's always that one woman who cuts the ground out from under even the wiliest man," he replied sagely. "Drives him crazy enough to forget the joys of being a bachelor."

"I wasn't aware that you were regretting your lost freedom," Mary commented ominously.

"I never had any," he chuckled. "You snapped me up before the other girls could get a chance at me. And I've always been glad of it," he added, pulling his wife down on his lap.

"Oh, you!" She gave him a push and a broad smile before going back to the stove. "But seriously, Mike, I'm worried about Jeremy. I think you should have a talk with him."

"Me? Are you kidding? That man could give me cards and spades in experience."

"You don't know it's a woman. Maybe he's . . . well, sick or something."

That thought creased Mike's forehead with concern. "Okay, I'll talk to him if I get a chance, but don't get your hopes up. Jeremy doesn't take kindly to anyone prying into his affairs."

Later in the day Mike spotted his employer strolling through the grounds. Jeremy's thumbs were hooked into the waistband of the tight jeans that rode low on his narrow hips. He was staring with great concentration at a rosebush, although Mike had a feeling that he didn't even see it.

"That's right, take a good look at what the deer did to that one," Mike said. "I'm telling you, Jeremy, if you

176

don't let me put up some fences, we're not going to have a flower left."

Jeremy grinned at the renewal of their old argument. "Deer have to eat too."

"Not my prize roses, they don't! What's the point of trying to keep things nice around here?" Mike warmed to his favorite subject. "You're just a pushover, do you know that? Let something bat its big beautiful eyes at you and you can't see it's nothing but a treacherous little thief!"

Jeremy's face changed, his eyes turning to green ice. "I didn't have to come home to be reminded of that," he ground out, turning on his heel and striding off.

Later in the day he sought out his caretaker to make an apology of sorts. "I'm afraid I'm a little on edge, Mike. I guess I've been working too hard."

Mike had seen him work twelve hours a day without showing signs of fatigue, but he avoided mentioning it now. "Maybe what you need is a change of pace," he remarked casually. "Lots of pretty girls around here would be glad to hear you're back."

Jeremy looked at him consideringly. "You may be right at that—about the change, I mean."

Mary was delighted when he told her he wouldn't be home for dinner. "You were all wrong about Jeremy brooding over a girl," she informed her husband. "He's taking Diane Barton out tonight. Does that look like he's pining over somebody else?"

"If he is, he's crazy. That little filly could hold *my* attention," Mike grinned.

"Just don't get any ideas, Mike O'Malley!"

"It doesn't cost anything to look," he teased.

"No, but it'll cost plenty if you touch," his wife warned.

Jeremy took Diane to the country club where there was dancing. They joined a large party of friends, who welcomed him back warmly. It was the life he was familiar with, the people he'd always enjoyed—but something was missing.

177

When he danced with Diane, she rested her dark curly head on his shoulder. "When are you coming home to stay, Jeremy?"

"Very soon I believe."

"I understand Washington is really exciting."

"I've been in Los Angeles for the last few weeks."

"Yes, we read about your investigation." She laughed. "Somehow I never pictured you as a detective, snooping around and finding out about people. I'll bet you're good at it though."

There were deep lines around his mouth. "Not very. As a matter of fact, I was an abysmal failure."

"That's not true," she protested. "The paper said you uncovered a whole scandal, and a television reporter—"

"Why are we talking about mundane things like corruption when we should be whispering sweet nothings to each other?" Jeremy interrupted smoothly.

Diane laughed. "I've always wondered what a sweet nothing was."

He drew her closer, murmuring in her ear.

"*Really,* Jeremy!" She pretended to be scandalized, but she didn't pull away.

The lights dimmed as the music changed to a slow, dreamy number. He molded her to his long body, smelling the scent of her heady perfume. Jeremy's hand wandered down her back, drawing her hips suggestively to his. Diane relaxed against him with a little sigh of pleasure.

The woman in his arms was seductive and pliant, beautiful and desirable, and Jeremy felt nothing. He groaned deep in his throat.

"What is it, Jeremy?" Diane cried in alarm.

"I'm sorry," he said without explaining. "I think I'd better take you home."

At breakfast the next morning Mary was full of expectation. "How was your date last night?" Her pleased anticipation faded at his grim expression.

"Just dandy." Before she could comment, Jeremy said,

"I'm going down to the office today to check on things. Don't bother about dinner for me."

Knowing he would probably skip it entirely, she considered protesting, but Jeremy had erected an invisible wall. Mary knew instinctively not to attempt to scale it.

Looking for a safe subject, she remarked, "You're getting to be famous. The papers are full of that investigation of yours. Especially since that girl television reporter —"

Jeremy stood up abruptly. "I'd better get going before the traffic gets too heavy."

In his company offices Jeremy relaxed for the first time. This was familiar territory, absorbing and satisfying. For once the hours flew by instead of dragging.

His secretary brought him a sandwich for lunch, and another one for dinner, remonstrating with him. "You really ought to take a break and go out for a hot meal, Mr. Hawke."

"No time, Jenny." He smiled up at her over an untidy pile of papers. "I've got to get this problem solved tonight."

"Well, can't I at least bring you something else to eat? A sandwich isn't enough for a big man like you."

"It's fine," he told her impatiently. "You run along."

He was absorbed in his work before she even got to the door. Jenny shook her head, knowing he would probably work half the night.

It was after eleven when Jeremy finally stretched and sat back with a satisfied look on his face. He was tired, but pleasantly so. Perhaps he would even sleep tonight. He'd watch the late news and then—Jeremy's sense of well-being started to ebb away as the image of a slender girl with sparkling blue eyes crept back to taunt him. With a muffled oath he grabbed his jacket and strode to the door.

He had just emerged from the shower when the phone rang. Frowning at the clock which told him it was ten minutes to twelve, he lifted the receiver.

179

"I hope I didn't wake you," Stretch said.

"No, I wasn't in bed yet. What's up?" Jeremy asked tersely.

"Well, I may be way out of line," his aide began hesitantly. "Rick said I was, but I still feel this is something I have to do."

"Will you kindly get to the point?"

"It's about Pippa."

"I don't want to hear about her." Jeremy's tone brooked no argument.

There was a short silence at the other end. "That isn't like you, chief."

Jeremy's voice was ominous. "You're meddling in things that don't concern you."

"That's true, but I've never known you to be vindictive."

Jeremy gave a short, bitter laugh. "I've never had quite this provocation."

"You do know about her then?" Stretch asked uncertainly.

"A little late, but yes, I know *all* about her."

"Well, I suppose I can understand how you feel."

A muscle jumped at the point of Jeremy's square jaw. "I don't feel anything one way or the other."

Stretch sighed. "I guess that's it then. You were the only one who could help her, but if you won't, then I'm afraid she's had it. I just wanted to be sure you knew."

"What are you talking about?" Jeremy asked sharply.

"About Pippa going to jail."

"Are you out of your mind? What for?"

"For refusing to tell the authorities Willie Maybeck's name."

Jeremy gripped the phone until his knuckles whitened. "Say that again!"

"You said you knew." Stretch was confused. "They hauled her up before a judge who ordered her to name him. When she refused, he gave her forty-eight hours to change her mind. The time is up tomorrow and I don't think she's going to crack."

"How about Woody Phelan?" Jeremy demanded. "The reporter who broke the story on the air. Why are they going after Pippa instead of him?"

"She evidently didn't give him the name." When Jeremy made an incoherent sound, Stretch said earnestly, "I know she played a rotten trick on you, but we have Maybeck all sewed up. Letting her go to jail seems pretty stiff revenge." There was such a long silence at the other end that Stretch asked, "Are you still there, Jeremy?"

"Yes, but not for long." Jeremy's voice was vibrant. "I'm coming back. Don't worry, I'll take care of everything."

His aide's anxious expression relaxed. "Shall I call Pippa and tell her?"

"No! I'll do it myself. And, Stretch . . . thanks."

Pippa had just fallen asleep when the insistent ringing of the doorbell woke her. She groaned, considering ignoring it and knowing she couldn't. Gloria had probably just figured out that the phone was off the hook.

When a glance at the clock told her it was a quarter past three, Pippa had second thoughts. Then she sighed, realizing the reason for this late visit. With her flair for the dramatic, Gloria had no doubt decided that Pippa had done away with herself. Her concern was touching, but she had just destroyed Pippa's chance for a few hours rest. She'd never get back to sleep now.

Without bothering with a robe Pippa stalked to the door, throwing it open. "Gloria, I wish you—" The words died on her lips as she stared up at Jeremy. "What are you doing here at this hour?" she whispered.

He stared back, as bemused as Pippa. "I couldn't get here any sooner."

His deep voice broke her trancelike state. Until now Pippa thought she must be dreaming. "I mean why have you come?" she faltered.

"I've been away. I just found out what's been happening—about you and the police."

A sense of disappointment so severe it was like an ac-

181

tual pain knifed through her. For a foolish moment she thought Jeremy had returned because he needed her as much as she needed him. Pippa wrapped her arms around her trembling body. "So you came here to gloat. Well, I suppose you're entitled."

He came inside, closing the door behind him. Knowing he wouldn't leave if she told him to, she switched on a lamp with an air of resignation. The light illuminated the many floral displays crowding the small room.

Jeremy was startled. "What the devil are all those?"

She gestured vaguely. "Just some offerings from friends."

He grinned suddenly. "It looks like somebody died—or won the Kentucky Derby."

Her answering grin gave rueful acknowledgment. As their eyes met, the amusement faded. Jeremy looked at Pippa searchingly. "Would you really have gone to jail tomorrow?"

"It isn't a question of would I—I'm going." She shrugged. "I don't have any choice in the matter."

"You could name Maybeck."

"Since I told them everything else they wanted to know, is that it?" she asked bitterly.

"I'm sorry about what happened in the newsroom, Pippa." There were furrows between his dark brows. "You'll have to admit you brought it on yourself though."

So he did still believe she was the one who had betrayed him. A feeling of hopelessness overwhelmed her. "Well, it's a good lesson for you." She tried for a flippant tone. It was the only thing that would sustain her. "Next time you'll know better."

"Why do you want me to think the worst of you?" he asked almost curiously.

"I don't care *what* you think." If he'd only go!

"No, I can see that," Jeremy said heavily. "I once thought you did, but that was all in my own mind. Don't worry, Pippa, you're not going to jail. I'll tell them what they want to know."

"You can't do that!" she cried. "You can't jeopardize all your work."

"All the evidence is in; they're processing the indictments now. The whole thing is over." He sounded almost disinterested.

So it wasn't concern for her that had prompted the offer. Pippa felt foolish at her passionate protest. "Well, I . . . I'm glad it turned out the way you wanted," she said uncertainly.

Jeremy's apathy vanished suddenly, consumed by the blaze in his green eyes. "That's a damn fool thing to say!"

She didn't pretend to misunderstand. "All right, so your pride is hurt because you were deceived by a woman." She turned away, her voice muffled. "At least you got payment for value received."

Jeremy grabbed her arm, whirling her around to face him. Both hands fastened on her shoulders as he shook her so savagely that her fine silky hair whipped around her pale face.

"I don't ever want to hear you say a thing like that again," he grated through clenched teeth. "You can pretend to yourself that those nights we spent together were all part of the job, but don't try to sell it to me! A woman doesn't respond like that in a man's arms unless she feels *something.*" When Pippa stared at him mutely, too breathless to speak, his hands moved up to frame her face. He held her so she couldn't move away. "Look at me and tell me that you never felt anything for me, that it was only sex between us."

"Why is that important to you? You got what you wanted."

"Answer me!" he grated.

Pippa's long eyelashes fluttered down to veil the only secret she had left. "I've lied to you before, what makes you think I'd tell you the truth now?"

"Why *did* you lie to me, Pippa?"

"I think that's pretty obvious. I would never have gotten in to see you in the first place if I hadn't."

"I wasn't talking about that. I mean later. How could

you go on deceiving me after we made love? After you let me find out everything else about you."

Pippa's heart started to thunder as she remembered all the things he knew about her—all the hidden places that had felt his enflaming caresses. Jeremy knew how to arouse her unbearably and fulfill her completely.

Her slender neck seemed unable to support her drooping head. "I wanted to tell you. Dear God, how many times I wanted to!"

"Then why didn't you?" he probed implacably.

"I was afraid," she murmured, almost too low to hear.

"Of what? What did you think I'd do to you?"

He continued to hold on to her, shattering Pippa's defenses with his remembered touch, the familiar scent of him, the warmth of that taut, lean body she longed for. A long quiver went through her as she gave up the struggle. What difference did it make anymore whose pride was salvaged? "I was afraid you wouldn't see me again."

"And then you wouldn't get the story?" he persisted.

Pippa's control suddenly snapped. "Stop it, Jeremy! Stop tormenting me! Do you have to hear it in words? Do you have to take everything from me? All right, I'll admit it. I fell in love with you—so crazy in love that I was terrified of losing you. I was afraid if I told you the truth, you'd put me out of your life, and I couldn't bear the thought."

Jeremy's arms went around her, crushing her so tightly against his hard frame that she almost felt like part of him. "My poor little Pippa. If I'd only known!"

She dragged herself out of his embrace, fighting the urge to take anything he would give her. "I don't want your pity," she declared in a shaky, but determined voice. "I'll get over this."

"I hope not for fifty or sixty years," he said gravely, although there was a twinkle in his eyes.

How could he make a joke of it when her heart was breaking? "Now that your macho ego is firmly back in place, would you please go?" She turned her back, unwilling to have him see the tears that threatened to fall.

He folded his arms around her, drawing her against him and burying his face in the curve of her neck. "You don't think I'd leave you now."

She tried desperately to break the grip of his strong arms around her waist. If he didn't stop touching her, she'd disgrace herself completely, beg for any small crumb of affection. "Please, Jeremy, I know you're trying to be kind, but it isn't necessary."

"Actually, what I'm trying to do is make love to you, but you're making it very difficult." His hands wandered up to cup the fullness of her breasts, circling the nipples with his fingertips.

"You . . . that's insulting!" she gasped, grabbing desperately for his hands. "Is this supposed to be a consolation prize?"

"It's the mark of a desperate man. If you don't turn around and kiss me, I won't be responsible for my actions." He swiveled her gently in his arms, cupping her chin in his hand to lift her face to his.

"Jeremy, I—"

"I thought reporters were supposed to be good listeners," he murmured.

His dark head bent toward her, his mouth reaching hungrily for her. An ache of fierce longing ran through Pippa at the remembered contact. She wanted this man so dreadfully! Nothing mattered except being in Jeremy's arms one last time. Pippa surrendered to the primitive need that filled her, returning his kiss with complete abandon.

He dragged his mouth away to mutter thickly, "My darling Pippa, I never knew anyone could mean this much to me."

She looked up at him wonderingly. "I thought you hated me."

He feathered her face with tiny kisses, running his hands restlessly over her body. "How could you ever think a thing like that? You must know how much I love you."

His mouth sought hers again, but Pippa held him off.

185

"Don't say things you don't mean," she begged. "It's enough to know you still want me. You don't have to pretend anything else."

He kissed her trembling mouth gently before scooping her up and carrying her to the couch. Holding her cuddled in his arms, Jeremy said, "There isn't ever going to be any pretense between us again, sweetheart. We've made each other miserable because neither of us had enough trust. But that's all over."

Pippa was afraid to believe him. "Do you really love me, Jeremy?"

Knowing that she needed to hear it in words, he said deeply, "I love you in every way a man can love a woman, my darling. When I thought you didn't care about me, life didn't seem worth living."

She flung her arms around his neck, clinging tightly to reassure herself. "I felt the same way! Oh, Jeremy, I was so afraid I'd lost you!"

His warm breath feathered her cheek. "How could you think I could ever stay away from you? Don't you know you're in my blood?"

He slipped the gown off her shoulders, sliding it slowly down her body so his eyes could devour its perfection. Still holding her on his lap, he trailed sensuous fingertips over the slope of her breasts, the flat plane of her stomach, the silken length of her thighs. But when his hand retraced the path, it lingered where her desire was strongest, stroking seductively until licking flames turned her liquid inside. Pippa arched her body into his with a tiny moan, mutely begging for release from his sweet torment.

He carried her into the bedroom, placing her tenderly on the bed. She watched him remove his clothes, quivering as the broad triangle of his torso tapered down to the pulsing proof of his manhood. He was like the statue of a Greek god, except that she knew he would be warm and firm against her.

When he clasped her in his arms, her hips sought his, moving against him with a passion that couldn't be delayed. He drew in his breath sharply at the scorching contact, pinning her down with the weight of his body. Jeremy's mouth closed over hers, his tongue probing with a driving masculinity as he filled every part of her, stoking the fire within to almost unbearable heights. When the leaping flames became too intense to rise any higher, Pippa reached the summit of sensation, her body vibrating with wave after wave of pleasure.

In the aftermath of the violent storm, they remained entwined for a long time. Dawn was starting to dissipate the darkness. Finally Jeremy stirred. "Don't let me go to sleep."

"Why not?" she asked drowsily.

"I have to see a judge this morning." When Pippa's eyes flew open, Jeremy kissed the tip of her nose. "How can we have a honeymoon if the bride is in jail?"

Incredulous joy filled her. Having Jeremy back had been enough of a miracle. It didn't seem possible that *all* of her dreams were going to come true.

"Do you think that same judge would marry us, or would that be too pushy?" he chuckled, smiling down at her radiant face.

"I think that's the least he can do," she murmured, raising her lips for his ardent kiss.

LOOK FOR NEXT MONTH'S
CANDLELIGHT ECSTASY ROMANCES®

All-new Candlelight Newsletter

An exceptional, *free* offer awaits readers of Dell's incomparable Candlelight Ecstasy and Supreme Romances.

Subscribe to our all-new CANDLELIGHT NEWSLETTER and you will receive—at absolutely no cost to you—exciting, exclusive information about today's finest romance novels and novelists. You'll be part of a select group to receive sneak previews of upcoming Candlelight Romances, well in advance of publication.

You'll also go behind the scenes to "meet" our Ecstasy and Supreme authors, learning firsthand where they get their ideas and how they made it to the top. News of author appearances and events will be detailed, as well. And contributions from the Candlelight editor will give you the inside scoop on how she makes her decisions about what to publish—and how *you* can try your hand at writing an Ecstasy or Supreme.

You'll find all this and more in Dell's CANDLELIGHT NEWSLETTER. And best of all, *it costs you nothing*. That's right! It's Dell's way of thanking our loyal Candlelight readers and of adding another dimension to your reading enjoyment.

Just fill out the coupon below, return it to us, and look forward to receiving the first of many CANDLELIGHT NEWS-LETTERS—overflowing with the kind of excitement that only enhances our romances!